Doom Town

DOOM TOWN

Gabriel Blackwell

ZEROGRAM
PRESS

Los Angeles, CA 2022

ZEROGRAM PRESS
1147 El Medio Ave.
Pacific Palisades, CA 90272
EMAIL: info@zerogrampress.com
WEBSITE: www.zerogrampress.com

Distributed by Small Press United / Independent Publishers Group
(800) 888-4741 / www.ipgbook.com

First Zerogram Press Edition 2022
Copyright © 2022 by Gabriel Blackwell
Cover image: Broken glass mosaic tile, decoration in Park Guell, Barcelona,
    Spain. Designed by Antoni Gaudí. Travel Faery / Shutterstock.com
Book design by Pablo Capra

PUBLISHER'S CATALOGING-IN-PUBLICATION DATA

Names: Blackwell, Gabriel, author.
Title: Doom town / Gabriel Blackwell.
Description: First Zerogram Press edition. | Pacific Palisades, CA : Zerogram
    Press, 2022.
Identifiers: ISBN 9781953409096 (paperback)
Subjects: LCSH: Married men--Mental health--Fiction. | Children--Death--Psy-
    chological aspects--Fiction. | Depression, Mental--Fiction. | Puppets--Fic-
    tion. | LCGFT: Domestic fiction. | Black humor.
Classification: LCC PS3602.L32576 D66 2022 | DDC 813/.6--dc23

Printed in the United States of America

Contents

He Describes a Feeling

I think I now remember that it first came on while we (*we* meaning my wife and I) were out looking at bowls, decorative bowls, I mean, the kind you put on your sideboard or buffet (we'd put ours on our sideboard, or the old tea cart we called the sideboard), *accent pieces* in other words, designed to remain empty, to take up space that might otherwise have been occupied by something more useful. This wasn't a thing my wife or I had ever meant to buy or have in our house; this bowl had been a wedding present from an uncle or second cousin, and, almost purely through its fragility and size, and even though neither my wife nor I especially liked the way it looked, we'd carried it with us through four moves. As little as we liked it, we couldn't bear the thought of it in a landfill somewhere, I guess, and we felt, despite ourselves and probably because, I thought, of its fragility, a strange need to care for it.

My wife and I were at the Macy's in the mall shopping for decorative bowls because our decorative bowl—the empty one, the wedding present, a deep blue with a white stripe or band around it and flower-like details inside—was broken. In fact, it had been broken long before, but we were, that day, a year or more later, finally getting around to replacing it. In the intervening year, the place where the bowl had sat had, very gradually, been taken over by unpaid bills and pieces of junk mail we hadn't thrown away yet, pink and green envelopes cautioning us to extend our warranties NOW, thick rubber and chrome car keys glued to huge postcards, pictures of checks with teddy bears and balloons on them, coupons for miraculous television antennae and disposable contact lenses—often, the mail wouldn't come for weeks, and then I would come home from campus one night to find our mailbox entirely full, crammed with junk mail addressed to our neighbors. My wife had said something about how cluttered the entryway always was, and how it didn't used to be like that, which meant, I knew, that, although she wouldn't be cleaning it herself or taking any steps to make it cleaner, she thought that it really ought to be cleaned, and the sooner the better. When the bowl had been there, somehow, I thought, the junk mail got to the trash or the recycling, and I remember sharing the naïvely hopeful thought that maybe having a new bowl would inspire a return to the tidiness we hadn't had since the bowl was broken. My wife didn't so much agree with me as she just acknowledged that this was the solution I'd decided on, and so the easiest way forward was to humor me by going with me to pick out a new bowl while explaining that she didn't really like decorative bowls and had never been able to find one that went with anything else in the house, and, briefly, very briefly, even this made me happy because it meant she was still thinking about the way our house looked and not about the way *her* house *would* look.

So, there we were, looking at bowls in the Macy's, still making that attempt to remain open to the possibility that, through the purchase of this bowl, we might somehow also be healing something we dreaded addressing so much we'd allowed it to fester. This was just after, at least, as far as I remember it, we'd stopped to look at—and we were, then, clearly only dragging our feet, putting off having to decide whether we would now acknowledge what it was we were really there to do, a thing I'm convinced we knew we wouldn't be able to do and were doing really only because we were already there, I mean already at the mall, at the Macy's, and the thought of admitting that we had come all this way on a weekday evening when both of us had work the next day, come all this way for no reason at all (in fact, worse, to deceive ourselves) would have been more dispiriting than I think we could have faced just then, stopping to look at these sheets in the way children suddenly become very interested in a feature of the pool they haven't noticed

before, like the depth of a particular spot or the darkness of the fil-
ter, just when their parents have made it clear that it is now time to
get out of the pool—various sets of higher-thread-count sheets in,
I think, maybe ivory or ecru or eggshell, some quiet hotel shade,
anyway. My wife furtively opened a few of the packages to feel the
sheets inside—you *had* to feel them, she'd once explained to me,
they expected you to feel them (even though there was, at this
Macy's, a small bright yellow sign saying *not* to open the packages
hanging from every other set of shelves just at eye level), and I'd
learned not to stand too close to her when she was trying to pick
out new sheets so that if someone walked by I could pretend to be
as shocked as they were that she was opening things she shouldn't
be opening—and I noticed that she was only opening packages
from the queen section, not the king section (our bed was a king),
and, when I pointed this out, she asked whether I thought the
sheets would be somehow less soft in a different size and why was
I standing over there, and this was when I decided that I really
needed to look at something, almost anything, else, but there was
absolutely nothing there that I needed: I didn't need an enameled
garlic press that looked like a clove of garlic with handles in the
shape of a woman's stockinged legs ending in red pumps; I didn't
need a stand mixer in a color that would complement the other ap-
pliances in the kitchen; I didn't need a new sauté pan or wok clad
in high quality steel or made out of a new compound; I didn't need
athletic socks or a moisture-wicking polo shirt in a fluorescent hue.
What I needed was, I recognize now, a way to justify having come
this far but not to go any further, a way to put off the decision that
would come later and as a result of which, I knew, I was likely to
come out the loser.

    In fact, now that I think about it, it was precisely at the
moment that, as I recall, I had finally gone from being simply
concerned with the pace of our selection process (of the bowl, I
mean) into what I would describe as an all-encompassing feeling
of desperate, frantic numbness (so much so that I picture myself,
in that moment, with my hand in my right pocket, on the point,

I mean, of pulling out my phone and checking the time, checking the weather for the day, checking, even—and this, I think, says it all, doesn't it?—my school email, which could only, at that time, on that day, have been depressing or worrying or depressing and worrying; still, I picture myself with my right hand in my pocket, even though I cannot, no matter how hard I try, remember what pants I would have been wearing, or whether I would have been resting more weight on one leg than the other, or what my other hand was doing, for that matter, and this is one of the dangers of language, this false sense of certainty in the presence of even one detail when really that one detail is vastly outweighed by the many unrecalled details, and which unrecalled details ought to alert us to the deception but which deception language instead conveniently covers up), when suddenly and for only the briefest of seconds, I thought again about the dog I'd seen get hit by the white SUV on our way to the Macy's, and this inescapable feeling of doom came over me. That was the start of it. That moment.

What I mean to say is, and I want to be clear on this point, what I mean is that I knew then—*at that exact moment*—that all, *all* of my efforts in that area, that is to say, in the area of attempting to heal the rift between my wife and myself (and why not be blunt? *all* of my efforts in *every* area, every single one), had been and would continue to be futile. There must have been precursors and explicit causes, must even have been glimmers of this feeling before that moment, but that moment, the one in the Macy's, seemed to mark some significant *turn*. Now, I thought, everything will get much worse, and nothing will get better, and this will be the way my life will go from now on. I remember, after it had first fumbled forward toward her, very possibly alarming my wife, my hand going up to my hairline, as if to check whether I was also going bald, and my wife, when she'd turned toward me, asking me why I was doing that, why I was holding my hand there, and not being able to answer her, which naturally made her angry, since she took this as an attempt to ignore her or shut her out, when in fact it was only a kind of expression of shock.

It wasn't, I should say, the utterly sickening pink and dark crimson of the Labrador's insides against its shiny black coat that had brought on this feeling of doom, and, though I can remember that image—I don't know how I'd ever forget it—it isn't really something I think about often; I just mean it wasn't the physical fact of the dog's death (or, really, the dog's *disintegration* in the face of the horribly violent impact) that brought on my feeling of doom, though, obviously, this would have been disturbing enough on its own, and even though I'm sure there are probably people who are now thinking it was probably exactly this confrontation with mortality that brought on my feeling of doom, that, even though I'm now saying that it very definitely *wasn't* that that brought on my feeling of doom, I'm only deceiving myself in doing so, but no, I think what disturbed me was something that other people, I thought, might not have even thought was worth thinking about, not in light of what had then happened, something that other people might not even notice or wouldn't be able to recall they'd noticed, a little thing, the littlest of things, I think, considering what had then happened, but something that nonetheless seemed significant to me.

I remember that just before I became aware of this feeling of doom, I was standing next to the floor lamps, looking across the dirty linoleum path at a series of displays of bowls and plates and flatware, next to which was my wife, seeming somewhat helpless, by which I simply mean that her whole posture, my wife's, I mean, her whole way of carrying herself in that moment indicated, to me, anyway, defeat, though now that I think of it, perhaps it only *really* indicated a deep and sincere interest in the display in front of her; at the time, I didn't think it would be possible for such interest to be sincere in any way, not because of my doubts in my wife but because such a shabby display as this particular one was, or, and this was really what was at issue, I think, for me, such interest in anything at this Macy's *at this particular moment*, a moment in which there were so many other things requiring our attention, though I recognize that this idea may have had more to do with my overall outlook, which, at that time—and I ought to be specific; I mean my outlook before the falling of this feeling of doom, though maybe I mean only my outlook in just the few instants before the falling of that feeling of doom—was not especially generous or particularly permissive, anyway, this feeling might have had more to do with my general outlook than it did with the real situation, and later, now, I could see that my wife was perfectly justified in giving her full attention to anything at all, anything else, even if only to take her attention away from those same things I thought made the paying of attention to anything else extremely difficult and that tended to make the person paying that attention seem uncaring or willfully oblivious, at least, to me, but then there was all the time she'd just spent comparing sheets.

Anyway, there was my wife in front of the bowls, looking defeated. I felt compelled to do something; I think, maybe, I worried someone would see the two of us and feel as though they ought to do the thing they would be thinking *I* ought to have done in the situation, like when a stranger waits a few seconds before saying *Bless you* or *Gesundheit* when the person who has just sneezed is obviously there with someone else but that someone else hasn't said anything. I feel more or less certain people would probably describe my demeanor in such situations as *cruel*; not that I intend to be cruel, just that, when seen objectively, I think my actions and thoughts in such situations are or seem those of a cruel person. If she feels defeated, my thinking goes, what can I do about it? Anything I do would only have the effect of making *me* feel better, because, in doing something, no matter how unhelpful it ultimately is, I could then see myself as having done something to help. In the moment, I didn't think about reaching out and putting my hand on the back of her left shoulder—a gesture I know mainly from films and television and not really one I can recall ever having personally experienced in life, but a gesture that, because of television and films, would, I think, probably be unmistakable to others, including, one guesses, my wife, as a sign of support (of a nonspecific and, honestly, meaningless kind, but recognizable as support or, really, recognizable as a desire (on my part) to *show* support, which, I think, is, in the case of so-called *emotional support*, really the same thing, which is why I think I can't bear to make such displays (I mean that, to me, they seem artificial and completely insincere and, over time, I think, cause more harm than effect good)) and a gesture that would tend to make me look at least familiar to others and signify to her that she isn't alone. Instead, as I've already indicated, I just did nothing or worse than nothing, since I know I don't like people staring at me when I'm not feeling my best, and here I was doing that to her, staring. Then, feeling I ought to do something, I *did* put my hand on her shoulder, I *did* reach out in a way that seemed appropriate as a spectacle if not sincere as an action, and she flinched a little, I could feel it, and I think the flinching must be what then put me in mind of the dog. But then the flinch wasn't really a flinch, because I hadn't actually touched her: I put out my hand and then pulled it back and put it up to my forehead and held it there, and, if she flinched, it would have been so slight I wouldn't have been able to see it (though if I'd been touching her, I guess I might have felt it), and so I don't know how the dog came to mind except through my imagining the flinch, which really, I think, says more about than it does about her. So she stood there looking defeated, and I stood behind her, undecided about whether to put my hand on her shoulder and suddenly feeling reproached by her even though she hadn't said or done anything that could possibly be considered reproachful, and she might not have even realized I was there at all, not really. But, although I was there looking at my wife going through something I'm sure was awful and that on its own ought to have been enough to bring on the feeling of doom, it wasn't her or her defeated posture—and this will just make me look even worse, I know—but my imagining of her reproach at my insincere attempt at comforting her in what I imagined to be her feeling of defeat and, in truth, it wasn't even my imagining of her reproach but rather the memory that my imagining of her reproach brought on, the memory of the dog, that brought about the feeling of doom, and, after all, I had no history with this dog, it wasn't our dog, it wasn't a dog I'd ever seen before that day, and anyway much worse had happened and much worse would, I thought, happen after, but it was the dog that, in that moment, brought on this feeling of doom.

In Which

A Dog, a Black Dog, Appears

This particular dog, this Labrador or Labrador mix, as a symbol or even an omen (maybe, in this case, omen is the better word?) or anyway as a precursor of my feeling of doom, this dog—and to make matters worse, from what I can recall, it had had an especially goofy look on its face when I first saw it in the yard of the house catty-corner to ours, with its tongue hanging out to one side, looking straight up, ears back, making it seem (and yes, I know this is anthropomorphizing) as though in awe of something—*this* dog, the one I remembered in that moment in the Macy's, seemed completely unlikely to bring on the feelings that remembering it actually did for me, but I think somehow the innocent look it had on its face had something to do with this. I mean that it made what happened to the dog that much more awful. I thought about what had to have been in this dog's head before it made its first steps into the road: At that moment behind my wife in the Macy's and for reasons I find I don't understand, I thought first that the dog must have seen or heard something on the lawn or in the trees across the way—another animal, maybe, or maybe I had, as usual, overthought things, and the dog had simply had some mindless impulse to run in that moment and so it had then started off to cross the street without thinking any further about why it was do-ing so. The dog had then stopped, just for a moment, I remember, at the curb, while a silver sedan passed dangerously close to it, and I think the dog's movements at *that* moment, maybe *those* were the catalyst for my feeling of doom—and not, I mean, what came after—because they suggested to me, and perhaps this was clear to me only in retrospect, standing behind my wife in the Macy's (though I think some hint of it must have reached me even in the moment I first saw the dog, because I can remember my stomach dropped when I spotted it down the block marking the half-empty bag of white sandwich bread and then sniffing at the mulch in the bed where the two babies had been buried), that some sort of realization must have followed quickly on this first impulse to run across, whatever that impulse had been and however strong it must have seemed to the dog. At the very least, I thought, this dog must have realized that the sedan that had just passed in front of it would, if it had moved any further forward, have killed it, and even if the dog hadn't fully realized what might have happened to it, it still couldn't have been oblivious to the sound and the force produced by the car, I thought, and so even if only perhaps at some deep, limbic level, and even if for only a fraction of a second, it must have thought better of that first impulse. The dog seemed, in that moment, just after the sedan had passed and I could see it again, frightened or alarmed by where it now found itself, as though, I thought, it had been dropped at the curb from above, as though it had just awakened from a dream in which it had been flying into this real and imminent danger, and so, like any sentient creature, the fear or alarm of travelling so quickly and unexpectedly to the very point of death could only have obliterated whatever thoughts it had had in mind the moment before, whatever thoughts those might have been. The dog must, at that moment and as completely as was possible, have forgotten its original impulse, as one might when, on getting up in the night and going to the kitchen for a glass of water, one is surprised by an intruder and so does not get the glass of water or even think of drinking or thirst until much, much later, and then only out of a totally separate set of impulses and perhaps only after being reminded that it is a necessary thing, drinking water.

I hope I'm not getting too far off track. It's just that this moment, this split second I'm talking about, is so important to what I'm trying to explain: The dog stood frozen at the curb for a moment, only for a moment, and then, devoid of that initial, more seemingly innocent impulse, it crossed the street or tried to cross the street sprinting, as though out of some secondary impulse, this one much stronger and springing quite naturally from a baser instinct, from, I would guess, the necessity fear provokes in all creatures to at least consider taking flight in the face of a threat, though in this case, the flight was *towards* danger rather than away from it. It was as though the dog were on springs—I mean, as though fear had pressed the dog back into a set of springs or coils and those springs or coils were now throwing it forward, hard. I briefly thought maybe instead the dog was reacting, in that moment, to its own failure to act on its first impulse in the previous moment, mentally pledging to do something incredibly stupid in defiance of its own good sense, though really what I think bothered me in the Macy's, what led, I mean, to this feeling of doom I've been trying to describe, is that I thought I realized then that my actions—in general, I mean, in other words, *all* of my actions, and I suppose, even, *all of my actions for most of my life*—indeed, I realized, the actions of everyone I knew, were all just the same sorts of mindless responses to the same sorts of base impulses. I mean that there I was, like the dog, looking across this street of sorts with some idea of a purpose, some stupid and probably incomprehensible-to-anyone-else reason I ought to cross—still, though, with some imagined but nonetheless compelling and closely held *reason* driving me to cross, to move forward—and then, when the horribly immediate possibility of my death brushed me back, I completely abandoned that reason for wanting to cross and resorted fully to my very basest instincts, those most cowardly and harmful to myself, finding myself then without reason rushing out in a direction I knew could only be horribly dangerous, rushing forward without any thought of the consequences for myself or anyone else. I realized then—I mean standing in the Macy's, looking at my wife's back—that I had earlier thought the dog ought to have just gone back, gone back to wherever it had originally come from (I mean, how stupid to insist on crossing the street, having forgotten the reason one had wanted to do it in the first place), and then, back in the Macy's, I wondered, even more briefly, about what this, this specific thought, might have meant about my mental state, about how debased I must have become, how far gone I already was. I didn't, I thought then, in the Macy's, want to return to some imagined state of innocence, I didn't think, which was, I knew, a completely fabricated state in any case, an unnatural state—I had, I hoped, so far resisted this impulse, baser than those I'd just thought of, the fears, the ones I had, I now realize, just accused everyone around me of acting upon, with everything I had. I could not, would not allow myself to want such a thing, I thought. Still, I remembered I'd thought, it was simply a fact that had the dog just turned around and gone back toward the boarded-up house instead of out into the street, it would never have been struck. It would still be alive. The fear provoking the dog not to retreat but instead to rush forward into certain death—*that*, that was the doom I felt, because, as I've said, I knew then that this was the fear governing every desperate, craven human action, which is to say, *every human action*, and this knowledge made me that much more afraid of everyone around me, indeed, of myself especially.

My wife—who, I then felt, was surely *also* a victim of this just-identified, unconscionable impulse towards death and destruction, not merely the death and destruction of others but also, and perhaps more importantly, of herself—my wife pointed out a blue, white, and green bowl, alone in a display of tinseled plastic grass just a shade darker than the border around the sign above her pointing the way to the bathrooms and the exits, with marshmallow rabbits playing among pastel paper flowers. As it was, though, I could think only of the sound of the impact, the sound of the tires squealing, that horrible and ugly thought I couldn't prevent: *That's just meat.* My wife had, I remembered, gasped, though, to her credit, she kept her focus on the road in front of her. *I don't know*, she said. *I don't like it*, my wife said. *I guess it's pretty much the same one, but I don't like it.*

At first, because of this feeling of doom and my thoughts of the dog, I stayed silent. Really, as I hope I've explained, I *couldn't* speak. It wasn't, as my wife would later imply, because I was ignoring her in that moment, or because, as she might have thought, I tended to ignore her most of the time, though I think I must have seemed, in that moment and from most other perspectives, to be ignoring her; really, I see now, it couldn't have seemed otherwise to her at the time, and I'm also sure this wasn't the first such instance of this rudeness and utter lack of respect for her I'd *seemed* to demonstrate, though I hope I was, nonetheless, not actually guilty of such rudeness and lack of respect. I see all of this, of course, but, as I've already tried to explain, I've found that, generally speaking, I'm also powerless—in the moment, I mean—to make things seem otherwise, to make myself seem to be acting otherwise. And anyway, no, it was not, I think, that I was ignoring her, not that I was intentionally not answering her in order to indulge in my own thoughts or simply petulantly, flagrantly pretending she didn't exist or hadn't spoken because I thought my thoughts were somehow more important than her words. No, instead, it was, I think, that I'd been so completely stilled by this feeling of doom brought on by my thoughts about the dog that I'd also been rendered completely helpless and silent in its wake, but, because of this stillness, helplessness, and silence, I couldn't say any of this in the moment. I was, in a word, I thought later—and this is strange; strange, I mean, that I thought this, that I would have come up with this thought—*penitent*. Like the earlier word *meat* my mind had somehow conjured when I saw what the white SUV had left behind of the dog, a word I immediately regretted thinking, I couldn't quite say why *penitent* was the word that occurred to me. It seems now a strange way to describe my feeling in the moment, maybe because, as I've thought since, penitence has to do with the choices one has made in one's past, while *doom*, the way I've since come to think of my feelings in that moment, the feelings, I mean, I had while in the Macy's facing my wife's back, after thinking of the dog before it had rushed out into the street, after thinking, I mean, of its impulses and their possible relationship to some inherent cravenness in humanity, has to do really with the inevitability of one's future, with *fate*, in other words. It's the latter, *doom*, that I think I was feeling in that moment, and yet, before this word came to me, the word *penitent* was all I could think. *Penitent*, I thought.

I have, I should say, in order to lift this feeling of doom, tried subsequently to imagine myself as someone who doesn't worry about the future, someone who has, I mean, held onto the illusion—it *is* an illusion—that his initial, seemingly innocent impulse is still the impulse that drives him forward (instead of the inhuman—but also of course *very* human, innately human—impulse that quite clearly *actually* drives him forward), but I find I can't will myself into that kind or that depth of ignorance no matter how hard I try, and so, in that moment, the moment I've been explaining, thinking about the dog in the Macy's, nothing seemed possible, including responding to my wife and thus, in short, helping to choose an appropriate decorative bowl or, for that matter, even seeming to be listening to her, by which I mean being a decent husband, by which, in this case, I guess I mean really a decent human being.

My wife, having a relatively short temper—fortunately, always before she was also a very forgiving person (she usually pretended to have an equally short memory though in fact she only has a selective one, and will nurture grievances large and small—frequently, in astonishing detail—for years)—said to me then, *This was* your *idea. The least you could do is give your opinion.* Somehow, this caught me off guard, and so I said, *It's crenellated?*, making with my left hand a meaningless gesture, a gesture as though pretending to swim as I remember it.

Later, at home, she would tell me that the bowl had looked like an empty pie shell. A green and blue pie shell with vines on it, she said, which—the fact that something that looked edible but was also, mostly, a color that, if it were edible, would indicate it shouldn't be eaten—was kind of gross. In talking about the bowl at all, I realized, she was offering up a truce of sorts; we could be civil to each other again if I would join her in talking about the bowl and its lack of suitability for the sideboard and, thus, its lack of suitability for us. And because I am, on occasion, an exceedingly stupid person, instead of simply agreeing with her, saying, *Yeah*, even though it was pretty much the same as the old one, because of the colors, it wasn't really that much like the old one (even though it very much was like the old one in shape, size, and even, largely, color, though in different proportions, and with the exception of the crenellations), I asked whether she thought it looked like a pie shell because of the crenellations. I don't think I meant to antagonize her or reopen old wounds, and I don't think I was trying to seem naïve or obtuse, though I'm certain I wouldn't have known if any of this had been the case, and I'd long ago decided that it wasn't worth the effort to try to find the reasons why I did or thought anything, since I would, I knew, simply lead myself around in circles without end. The dog, for instance: Had I seen its situation the way I saw it because I *already* felt doomed? That is to say: Had I seen things as they really were in the case of the dog and its impulses or thoughts, or only as I thought I wanted them to be?

(I felt certain I wasn't trying to continue the fight I also felt I had never consciously engaged in, much less started, though, in truth, I don't know. My wife had grown frustrated with me when I tried, long before all this, to explain my complete and utter loss of faith in words and language—it was a change to my way of thinking that, I thought, explained why I was then not apologizing for something I'd done, I don't remember what, and I'd hoped this explanation would somehow end the argument we were then having, whatever that argument had been about, but I remember that, as I tried to explain this change to my way of thinking to her, I started to feel ridiculous, started to see my whole rationale as itself ridiculous, and I realized that, in explaining this loss of faith, I was very much acting in bad faith and according to principles I'd decided to abandon and that were, in fact, the very principles I was, at that moment, attempting to explain were principles according to which one should never act. I could see in her expression that she saw what I'd been saying was, as an excuse for my bad behavior, completely inadequate. Although I can't remember what brought this on, what specific stupid thing I'd said or done, I do remember we didn't speak the rest of that day, and that wouldn't have been so strange, not at that point in our relationship, if not for the fact that she also didn't leave the house, and we both remained where we had been, sitting at the kitchen table, silent. (I was, I remember, a little afraid to get up, though for what reason I couldn't say.) My wife, I'm sure, could, without hesitation, recount exactly what I'd said or done that had led to this argument, though I feel bound to say that I've never truly believed in the absolute faithfulness of these recountings (not that I'd ever dream of telling her this), nor am I certain that their fidelity is all that important, really: rather, it is, to her, the confidence she has in her version of events that matters most. *She* believes that she's telling the truth, and so what she says seems (to others, and to herself) true.)

A Traffic Jam Is Mentioned

We, my wife and I, did not, in other words, purchase the bowl that evening, and we left the Macy's empty-handed, as I'd guessed we would. I'd guessed we'd leave the Macy's empty-handed not because I thought the bowls we'd find would be inappropriate or inadequate, or because I thought *any* decoration we found would be inappropriate or inadequate, but instead because of a moment that had passed between me and my wife earlier in the week, while discussing this particular trip to the Macy's—the timing of the trip, I mean, the necessity of it. I'd mentioned the bowl—that is to say I'd mentioned I'd found what looked like the same bowl, as far as I could remember the bowl's original, the wedding present (it had, again, by then, been over a year since this original, wedding-present bowl had broken and the shards of it had been thrown out, and I couldn't, more than a year later, find a picture of the bowl or even a picture in which the bowl could be seen (though, to be fair, I didn't try especially hard)), and had asked my wife whether we shouldn't go and look at this possible replacement, maybe also bring it back to the house and put it in the same spot the old one had occupied, though I'm sure I didn't use those words and possibly tried to communicate some other sentiment altogether, all in an effort (misguided, probably, and definitely transparent, as all such efforts inevitably are) to appease my wife, who, moments before, had become blindingly angry with me for some small and probably indetectable transgression (indetectable to me, I mean, indetectable in that I hadn't noticed I was even doing it, though, as she would later suggest, correctly, I guessed, had she done it to me,

I would have felt just as aggrieved as she had), probably, knowing me, the offense of simply not listening to her, that is, not paying attention to what she was saying or doing, and probably, knowing me, not paying attention to her because I'd been paying attention to the woodworking show she thought I'd turned on solely for background noise or distraction and that I couldn't admit, not yet, not to her, to actually *wanting* to watch, hoping to pick up some tips, and which woodworking show I was, at the moment she spoke to me, as far as I can now remember, trying really hard to hear—I may even have displayed some signs of being annoyed when she'd said whatever it was that she'd said because I was actually trying to watch the show and wasn't paying attention to her, and it's entirely possible what she was saying was, ultimately, much more important than what the host of the woodworking show was saying (in any case, I no longer recall what the host was saying, even in essence), and, because I can't now remember what he, the host of the woodworking show, was saying and because, apparently, I never knew what my wife was saying, the moment stands out in memory mainly for the anger I can remember my wife expressing immediately after it had passed. In any case, and although I hadn't been paying much attention to her before her anger manifested itself, I definitely *was* paying attention to her after it had, and so I sought some way of appeasing her without bringing up the subject of what I'd just missed in what she was saying, without, I mean, asking her what she'd just been saying and what, ultimately, she was so upset I hadn't heard. Holding up my phone, I said, *This one's like the bowl that used to be on the sideboard*, trying to avoid referring to our son altogether, since that tended to end conversations between us. She refused to take my phone, though, and refused also to look at me, maybe mirroring my attempt to pretend whatever had happened hadn't, in fact, happened by now pretending that what was now happening wasn't, in fact, happening. It was, in short, a perfectly reasonable and also, of course, perfectly childish—appropriately childish, I mean; it's not as though she was the only one acting childish—response. *You know, the one we got from your uncle? Right? For our wedding?*

Now you want to talk? she asked. *Now it's OK not to pay attention to this stupid show?* This wasn't what I meant, of course—I would have preferred to watch the woodworking show, especially because they had, just then, moved on to mortise and tenon joints, or at least this is what I remember seeing out of the corner of my eye, and then there's the fact that I would have preferred to watch really anything at all on television rather than have the conversation I knew we were about to have—but I couldn't say that, of course, not then, and I was still wary of directly addressing what had, or at least what I thought had, just incited her anger, in the interest of, or so I thought, moving us entirely past the subject and onto something else.

You were talking about the sideboard the other day, I reminded her. *Weren't you saying that maybe we ought to put the shorter bookcase in there, so that it won't just keep collecting junk mail?* This was true, or at least I thought it was true; she had complained that the sideboard was collecting junk mail—we'd both noticed it, and I've already mentioned it here. This conversation, though, rapidly devolved into an argument, as I knew it would, though I think—or rather, thought, as future events would show—that I successfully kept this argument somewhat shorter than it might have been by insisting on my innocence (I hadn't heard her only because I was watching the show, not because I didn't care what she was saying; of course it can't have escaped my wife's attention that these two things weren't mutually exclusive, indeed, that they were, in fact, very closely related) and by returning, again and again, to the bowl, until finally, exasperated or else just exhausted, my wife relented and said she could go and look at it on Wednesday, after work, though she knew that Thursday was likely to be a very long teaching day (the last day of classes, the day students came to my office to cry or complain), or probably, I thought then and still, at some level, think now, really *because* she knew that Thursday was likely to be a very long teaching day. I had no real choice but to say OK.

On the way home from the Macy's—my wife refused to be in the car when I was driving and so she drove us everywhere we went together—and while we were stuck in traffic, this same argument flared up again, though I'm sure it really only flared up again because we were stuck in the car together and because we had nothing else to do and nothing to distract us from each other and probably because the traffic was—understandably, I think—finally getting to my wife. *What's going on up there? Why aren't we moving?* she asked, although it was clear that she wasn't asking me and didn't expect or even especially want me to respond. She said this, in fact, I thought, because she was so angry she could no longer talk directly to me, and had momentarily given up on resolving anything. Of course, inevitably, I was thinking at the time, it would be some poorly planned construction that was at fault, it would be some dumb thing the local or state police had done or failed to do, like the time they'd closed the left lane at exactly the point in the road where the far right lane ended, meaning that there were *two* lanes trying to merge into the center lane at exactly the same spot. They'd done this, I remember, for a road crew that was working a mile and a half ahead of the start of the lane closure, a road crew that wasn't even working on the road itself but off the shoulder. (These are details that shouldn't have stayed with me, and the persistence of the memory of this—and my strong feelings about it—is one more reason I wouldn't have been driving then, though of course additional reasons weren't necessary.) We could see brake lights all the way up to the bend in the road, maybe half a mile ahead. I remember thinking that I would feel better somehow if it was an accident—at least then it would have some obvious justification—and then thinking that this was a cruel and cynical way to think, but the cars ahead of us, for as far as I could see, didn't move at all through three, then four, then five cycles of the light at the next intersection. I would have been infuriated if I'd been driving, but my wife didn't seem to get any angrier. It was clear that she was upset—mainly, I think, with me—but she wasn't cursing the drivers passing us by going up on the curb the way I would have and she wasn't saying deeply stupid things as I might have, like the thing about hoping the stoppage was because of an accident. Instead, she shifted in her seat, trying to force my hand, which was, just then, resting on the outer edge of her thigh, to twist in a way that would be uncomfortable, forcing me, I think, to lift it without making it seem as though she was actually pushing it away. An ambulance raced past us, on the other side of the road, and then a helicopter flew overhead, and my wife turned down the radio; we could hear sirens coming toward us from different directions.

To distract her, I think, I tried to tell my wife the story of Moremi, the queen of Ilé-Ifè, who'd allowed herself to be kidnapped by the Ìgbò so as to learn all she could about the Ìgbò, so that she'd know how to stop the Ìgbò from killing her cousins and raiding Ilé-Ifè. Her husband, the king, heir to the father of the Yoruba, when he saw she was determined to go through with this risky plan, hadn't raised a finger to stop her, I told my wife, quite the opposite, I said—he had even taken Moremi down to the stream and shown her how to pray to the god of the stream, and what words to say. *I will make you the richest sacrifice I can if my mission is successful,* the king instructed his wife to say. When the Ìgbò came next, they took Moremi away with them, and, once she was back at their village, she saw that what the Yoruba warriors had been afraid of was nothing more than grass and bamboo weaved together, I told my wife, who was already, at this point, rolling her eyes and sighing loudly, and if I were a different, more solicitous or even simply self-aware person, I might have stopped there, but instead I told her that in truth they were just masks that made the men wearing them look bigger and more frightening. Their weapons were better than those the Yoruba used, I said, but they were made out of things the Yoruba had, too, and anyway, as Moremi soon saw, all that was necessary to defend against the Ìgbò was a simple torch or even an ember, to set the Ìgbò's grass-and-bamboo on fire, and then, I explained, the threat of their raids would be gone. Moremi was very beautiful, and so, I said, feeling

self-conscious about why I'd included this detail when I could have
easily left it out—my wife didn't care, couldn't have cared—the
chief of the Ìgbò took her as his concubine, and Moremi stayed
with the chief of the Ìgbò just long enough that she learned all she
had come to learn about the Ìgbò, and then, because she was also
very clever, she escaped, I told my wife, and returned to Ilé-Ifè and
her husband.

And it is at this point that things became complicated, I told
my wife, and I could see she was only just barely holding herself
together, her mouth set and her eyes focused near the horizon,
carefully avoiding mine, though at the time I remember thinking
it would be better for her to be distracted by anger at me than to
be focused on her frustration with the traffic; sometimes, for reasons I've never understood, I *wanted* her to be angry with me even
though I knew it could only weaken our relationship; I prefer to
think of this as self-sacrifice, though I think there's something mas-
ochistic in me, too. Things were complicated, I said, though now
my voice was shaking a little, because even though Moremi made
the *richest sacrifice* she could think of, sheep, cows, swans—none
of it satisfied the god of the stream. The king, her husband, told
her that the only sacrifice the god would accept now was their son,
her only child, and so she had no choice but to sacrifice him to
the stream, and so she stood, weeping, in the stream and held him
under, this boy she hadn't seen for months while she lived with
the Ìgbò, almost a year, and just then my wife slapped me, hard
but a little clumsily, with the back of her hand, basically really a
punch, only with an open hand, and then, after a period of silence,
I remember the traffic finally started moving. I'd wanted to tell her
that even though Moremi thought she'd sacrificed her son, in fact
he wasn't dead—this was the part of the story I'd wanted her to
hear—and that the god of the stream had made a ladder to heaven
out of the bones of the animals she'd sacrificed to it for her son to
climb, but after she'd slapped me or punched me, neither one of
us said anything.

Later, after reading her post, my wife explained that there

had been what the woman with the police scanner and the active imagination described as *an incident of road rage* on the bridge; one driver shot his pistol into the other driver's car window, and the car that had been shot into then rammed the side of the shooter's car, causing it to spin out and break through the warning barrier on the bridge. The shooter's car had been stopped by the emergency railing, although, when we passed the scene, the car's rear passenger side tire was hanging off the bridge, and it looked like the front passenger side wheel might have been hanging off, too. The car that had been shot into had already been towed away, and all of this happened at night, so we didn't see the blood on the road or in the car, but I did see it later, when my wife showed me the woman with the police scanner's post. In the comments below the post, there were rumors that the man who'd been shot at had actually forced the shooter out of his car and tried to bite off the skin on his left arm, but I couldn't find any evidence of this when I read the news accounts of what had happened and I wondered where these people had heard it, if it had actually been printed somewhere. They blamed the whole thing on the synthetic drug that had been in the news lately, the most recent one, even though there was no evidence that this drug was being sold or abused anywhere in the area, and even though it later turned out this drug had had nothing to do with the incident.

A Stranger Is Mentioned

My wife had, as long as I'd known her, had trouble sleeping, a condition that long predated our son's death but that seemed to change and become substantially worse after it, taking an unusual and even disturbing form, in that her trouble was no longer not sleeping—because, to any observer, it would have been apparent that she was sleeping—but instead that she woke feeling as though she hadn't slept (even though, again, she had) and would, when we were better disposed toward each other or when she just needed to vent, tell me—as though they were events that had actually happened—about what I felt could only have been vivid, very vivid, dreams, which obviously would themselves have been evidence of her having slept, and which I felt *must* be dreams because they typically involved me doing things I had no memory of doing, things I felt were things I wouldn't have done under almost any circumstance, and which I therefore felt were things I hadn't, in fact, done, *couldn't* have done, and which must therefore be things my wife could only have dreamt of, not, in other words, things that had happened. To be clear, these weren't things like flying or changing into an enormous lizard monster; they were relatively mundane things, things like, for instance, saying strange things to her in my sleep, when, she said, she could *see* I was asleep, asking her questions that seemed, she told me, like challenges to her, questions or challenges that were, besides, just vague enough to keep her mind occupied all night trying to figure out why I was asking them, questions or challenges like *What were you doing?* in which question or challenge the use of the past tense, she claimed, was more surprising, mysterious, and, ultimately, disturbing than the substance of the question itself, and which past tense alone was enough to keep her from falling back to sleep or getting to sleep in the first place: *were*? I was not and am not someone who talks in their sleep, though I realize, being myself asleep at the time, I'm probably not a particularly convincing authority on the subject. Still, my wife had never mentioned this fact to me before, not after years of us sleeping together, and no one else who had ever slept in the same room with me had mentioned it, either, not until my wife did. Anyway, she said, there were more disturbing things I'd done (more disturbing than my questions or challenges), times she'd awakened to find me standing above her, not necessarily standing *over* her, just very close to her, on her side of the bed. She accused me of this on several occasions, in fact, I remember. I always agreed that such a thing would of course be horribly disturbing, but I also maintained I had no memory of doing such things, and, when I woke on those mornings—I always woke long before my wife—I would see her sleeping seemingly peacefully, and so when she would tell me that she hadn't been able to sleep at all the night before because she'd fallen asleep for maybe an hour or two and awakened to find me standing above her and then of course couldn't get back to sleep, I'd think, first, that I couldn't remember doing any such thing; second, that it would be completely out of character for me to have done something like what she was telling me I'd done; and, third, that she'd seemed to be sleeping pretty well when I woke up, maybe two or even three full hours before she got out of bed, so—and this I didn't say, not to her—I found it difficult to believe that she hadn't slept, and therefore had a hard time believing I could have been the cause of her sleeplessness. She, however, was absolutely certain—I had spoken to her in my sleep, I had stood above her while she slept, I had rolled over and, with a strange and horrible expression on my face (how could she see my expression in the dark? I thought; our room was very dark with the shutters nailed shut (the landlord had done this for one of the hurricanes and then had never come back to open them up again after the storm's threat had passed and we'd left them like that in the bedroom (though we opened the others), for the privacy and for the darkness)), had stared, for what seemed like hours, at her, as she tried to sleep—and this certainty persisted despite all of my denials, and, during this period, the subject came up nearly every morning (why was I doing this? shouldn't I see a doctor? she didn't like it), and eventually I came to feel sorry for her despite myself, and came very close to taking responsibility for something I couldn't and didn't believe I'd done or even was capable of doing, purely to ease her obvious distress.

I also, I should probably say, doubted her accusations because after all *she* was the one who talked in her sleep, often saying perfectly intelligible sentences that nonetheless made absolutely no sense (*I don't know Travis*, I remember she'd said one night, and it was true—neither she nor I knew anyone named Travis, as far as I knew), and it was she who had, when we'd first moved in together long ago, told me she would sometimes watch me sleep while she was lying there awake, unable to sleep. The things she was accusing me of, in other words, were things I either knew she'd done or that she'd told me she'd done or that, purely on the basis of the things she'd reported she'd done, weren't out of the question for her to have done, all now interpreted as something sinister rather than something loving because—I couldn't avoid the conclusion—*I* was the one doing them and not her. She was disturbed, I was at fault, and she brought these things up so that, I felt, she had a convenient way to express her displeasure with me: It was my fault she couldn't sleep.

I say all of this to explain why, when she told me I'd been, as she put it, *waiting for her in the dark, like a creep*, after she'd gotten up in the middle of the night to go to the bathroom, I instinctively denied it, and, even after searching my memory, I couldn't remember any such thing happening, neither standing in the dark on her side of the bed, waiting for her to come back from the bathroom, or her fright at finding me there. In fact, I thought, I'd slept well the night before, couldn't remember getting up even once—and this was unusual because I'd rarely had such a restful night, often in fact getting up in the middle of the night because my wife was talking in her sleep or, more frequently, because I'd had too much water just before bed—and so the whole thing just seemed like yet another example of her remembering what she'd dreamt (I could think of no other possible explanation) but believing that what had happened in that dream was, instead, what had happened in reality. The only other possibility was that she was making up strangely elaborate and improbable lies so as to have someone to blame for her feelings of exhaustion, I felt.

Because this was a common enough occurrence—though it didn't happen *every* night, it might have happened once every two weeks or so—neither of us thought much about it, I think, or at least we didn't talk about it after she'd mentioned that it had happened again. But when, the morning after what she claimed had been another sleepless night, the second one in a row, she asked me why I'd gone into the attic in the night, I took it as a sign of some otherwise inexpressible upset or discontent on her part (or else—and this I didn't really want to consider, because of what it would then mean in terms of the initiative and energy I'd be expected to expend, and the conflict it would provoke—a serious mental disturbance), which is to say that, because I didn't accept it as even possibly an account of something that had actually happened—I *hadn't* gotten up in the middle of the night; I *hadn't* gone up into the attic; the attic, as far as I knew, would require a ladder to get into, and we didn't have a ladder—I thought of it only as yet another one of these strangely real dreams she was having, an accusation against which my best defense was that I had, I thought, slept soundly the night before, and could remember nothing at all of what she was telling me I'd done, and besides, this was so obviously an accusation that, I thought, fit perfectly into this continuing pattern of accusations whose real source neither one of us was eager to discover and whose substance was completely fabricated.

It was surprising, then, when, one night, *I* woke to hear footsteps, the sound of heavy soles hitting our hardwood floors and then being muffled by our carpets—someone was walking around in our house when no one should have been walking around in our house, at a time, in other words, when my wife and I (I looked and, in the faint light from the clock, I could see she was there beside me, or at least there beside me was a lump in the shape of her in the bed, covered) were in bed. I say it was surprising, though really it was frightening. I was frightened. I knew I could get up, knew, that is, I could verify that the sounds I was hearing were real, that there were in fact shoes on feet in another room of the house making this noise, but, like my wife, I guess, I preferred not to do this, telling myself it was, as my wife's report had been, merely the product of my overheated imagination and couldn't be the noise made by a real person moving around in another room of the house. It was, I remember, warm that night, even with the air conditioner going, and I moved my arms out from under the sheet where they'd lain and felt I would have to get up and go out into the hall and down the hall to the bathroom—I had to pee—but instead I was terrified into stillness, thinking, *I can't get out of bed; I can't even think about leaving the bedroom, not with a stranger in the house*, and only my terror and the perfect stillness it seemed to demand kept me from reaching across the bed and waking my wife. Earlier, I'd thought: *If she really thought it was me out there making those noises, why didn't she just check the bed next to her? Why had she simply assumed it was me?* I'd felt it was another piece of evidence that helped to prove that what she'd heard wasn't real, I mean, but now that I lay there trying to find the will to shake her awake, now, I thought, I understood her better.

In Which
Evidence Is Mentioned

The sound—what I'd thought were footsteps—stopped, and was then replaced by a different, quieter sound, a liquid sound, and I think just the fact of that change was enough to release the tension that held me in place so that I could finally get up and out of bed and walk down the hall heading towards the living room rather than back further into the house, towards the bathroom, even though I could only have still very much needed to pee. I remember I couldn't decide whether I ought to make noise, to scare whoever or whatever it was that was making these noises in the living room into leaving, or if I should instead be perfectly silent, so that whoever or whatever was making these noises in the living room wouldn't know I was awake and so that I could, before deciding what else to do, see who or what they were. When I got to the end of the hall, I could see that the front door was open—not unlocked but actually *open*, standing wide open, and the room, I remember telling the policeman, smelled strange, a little like lighter fluid, maybe, but also like a person who hadn't bathed in a long time, though my wife would later, when I was telling all of this to the very tired policeman who finally showed up just before sunrise, many hours after we'd called 911, make a noise with her mouth and nose that meant, I knew, that what I was saying about this smell was ridiculous and probably inaccurate. There wasn't anyone in the living room when I turned on the light, but a woman's blouse—not one of my wife's—was lying next to the sofa (my wife would tell the policeman it was a maternity blouse, probably because neither he nor I seemed to have noticed that detail), and, later, after we'd moved the sofa, we found a condom wrapper next to the blouse or where the blouse had been when I'd found it (before, without thinking, I'd moved the blouse to the back of the sofa, to get it off the floor so no one stepped on it).

I was the one who called the police; though I'd wanted to check to make sure nothing had been taken first, my wife insisted I call immediately after I'd explained the situation to her. I hadn't needed to wake her—she'd come into the living room behind me while I was still trying to decide how close to get to the blouse on the floor—and this was good, because I can recall (again, because this was a detail I gave to the policeman) that I felt worried about turning my back on the living room. It had taken me what had seemed like hours to move myself just from the end of the hall to the front door, to close it; I was, I remember, worried not only about what would happen if I tried to cross the room, but also worried about trapping whoever or whatever had been in the house with my wife and me in the house with my wife and me. *Call them now*, my wife said, startling me. *It'll take them forever to get here*, she said, and to her credit, it did take them the rest of the night to arrive, which meant that, by the time the very tired policeman came to the door—after what had seemed like an eternity of the police car sitting outside, parked next to the curb in front of our house, my wife and I looking out the front windows at it and wondering when the policeman or policewoman would finally get out and walk up our driveway—my wife and I were both exhausted and in that state where it seems impossible that you're still awake, but, because the sun has come up and it's the time you would normally be getting up, you can't help but *feel* awake and unable to go back to sleep. While we waited for the police to show up, I remember I'd started looking around the room, moving the big green chair, looking under the coffee table for anything else that might have been left behind, remembering also to look for the hospital's reimbursement check (a check they would later claim had been an overpayment, and for which sum they then billed us again, with interest) that had come in the mail but that we hadn't cashed and that was sitting on the sideboard in the pile of mail where the decorative bowl had once been, remembering to look for my wife's work phone she'd left plugged in next to the toaster to charge, the set of silver in the oiled mahogany box my wife had inherited from her great-aunt, the box of papers with our tax returns, every few minutes thinking of something else that might have seemed worth stealing, but everything was where it normally was and nothing was missing, and my wife eventually told me to stop, sit down, that I was messing things up for the police, that surely they'd want to see the scene of the crime as it had been when the crime was committed (what was the crime? breaking and entering, I guessed, but I wondered why someone had bothered to break in only to not then take anything), and this made sense to me and made me feel ashamed of myself, but it also turned out to be completely untrue, since, when the very tired policeman arrived, he didn't dust for prints, take pictures, or do any of those things one sees on TV. Instead, he stood outside the front door for a while, on the patio, writing down parts of what my wife and I said and ignoring other parts of what my wife and I said, and then he flipped the cover of his metal clipboard closed, came in, glanced at the sofa and around the living room, said a few things in code into the walkie-talkie attached to his shoulder, and asked us if there was anyone else in the house.

The very tired policeman also asked what my wife and I did for a living, and when I said I taught at the university, he'd wanted to talk about his daughter, apparently just then a junior in high school hoping to apply for early admission to the university—there was some scholarship he kept referring to but which I'd never heard of, a private scholarship of some kind that seemed to have to do with the student's *devoutness*—when he first mentioned this, I could feel my wife staring at me, no doubt thinking I would say something negative about it, about this scholarship based somehow on neither need nor academic merit, but instead on the judgment of some falsely pious person of the student's blind adherence to a set of principles first set down as part of a fiction and ever since continually twisted and perverted to suit the needs of those who happened, at those moments, to be in power. I said none of this, though, in another situation—and if our relationship had been other than what it then was—I might have made a comment to my wife about the incoming class after the policeman had left. All the while, codes came in over the walkie-talkie on the very tired policeman's shoulder, some shouted.

My wife, maybe out of concern that the conversation might take a bad turn if I were left alone with the policeman, told him about all of the other nights she'd heard footsteps in the house, specifically mentioning the night when she thought I'd been looking down at her, but which now seemed more likely to have been someone else looking down at her, a stranger looking down at her. I remember thinking the officer looked uncomfortable during this part of the conversation, though it might just have been something he was hearing over his walkie-talkie, and he asked again whether there were other people in the house. I told him about the Uber driver living behind us in the mother-in-law, but only after not doing so the first time the very tired policeman had asked, worrying he might go and wake the Uber driver to interrogate him. *I really don't think he had anything to do with this*, I told the policeman. I remember I tried to ask whether this kind of thing, *breaking and entering, I mean*, I said, ever led to anything more serious, like robberies or violence, but I phrased my question in a weird way—I was exhausted—and the very tired policeman excused himself and told me they would make an effort to be more of a presence in the neighborhood, and I knew this meant they were stretched thin as it was and weren't likely to do much for us while there were violent deaths happening every day, women's bodies found hidden under floorboards and in freezers, random stabbings in the parks, a hanging, the old man who'd rammed pedestrians at the Saturday farmer's market, things that were becoming so commonplace they sometimes didn't even make the news the next morning and were only reported on later, as part of a more comprehensive piece on the so-called *uptick in violent crimes in the area*. Having finished his notes, the policeman, whose name I don't remember and feel certain I never really knew (though it must have been stitched on him somewhere and he surely also said it aloud at some point) and who had had dirty fingernails and a small dark patch on the back of his uniform near the beltline (blood, my wife later told me, probably fresh, though I have no idea how she would have known this detail), then left, and my wife and I cleaned up the mess I'd made before he'd arrived, not really knowing what to do with the blouse and the condom wrapper. The officer hadn't taken either one with him, I said, so maybe they weren't really helpful as evidence. But, I said, maybe it was just that he wasn't a detective, and maybe later a detective would come and want to look at them. Should we keep them? My wife told me we didn't have anywhere to put them—she didn't want them in the house, and we couldn't put them in the garage, where they would get ruined, at least ruined for the purposes of evidence. And wouldn't the policeman have done something with them if he was going to ask someone else to look at them? Like put them in a Ziploc or something? He wouldn't have just left them like that if they were important, we agreed.

On
Crenellations

But now I'm not sure it *was* sleep-related; my feeling, in the Macy's, facing my wife's slumped back, of an impending doom, as I think I meant to say, might instead have had something to do with the mood, the funk, lingering from the encounter with the police that morning. (The morning of the day we went to the Macy's, I mean, the morning, in other words, of the day during which I'd seen the dog get hit and then later, the same day, thought of the dog getting hit while in the Macy's shopping for a decorative bowl with my wife.) I don't mean to blame the police for the falling of my feeling of doom there in the Macy's; no, I think it's more likely that the lingering mood from the break-in and the apparent suicide and the police had more of an effect on the argument my wife and I had later that day than they did to my feeling of doom in the Macy's, but I guess I also think they ought to be at least mentioned in their proper context, the context, I mean, of the feeling of doom and its most proximate (proximate in time) causes.

In any case, it was clear my wife took my question about crenellations as a further provocation rather than as a sincere effort to respond to what she'd just said, which, as I've already said, was anyway less the starting of a conversation than, I think, an offer of a temporary truce. I'm not sure she shouldn't have taken it that way—as a provocation, I mean; though I wasn't conscious of intending it that way, how else could she have understood my insistence on responding in the way I did rather than acknowledging that she'd offered up a cease-fire? It isn't as though I wasn't aware of how I must have come across to her, only that I also knew what

I was thinking at the time and so I can supply that bit of information now, whereas, in the moment, I couldn't or wouldn't do so to her, and instead had said what I'd said—on the surface, then, and to her, I'm sure, seeming to ignore the very real and apparently sincere offer she'd just made and choosing instead to continue to antagonize her, though in truth I was only distracted by my feeling of doom and not focusing on the conversation I was having and so also not being careful about what I was saying. I couldn't think of a single story that I thought would be appropriate, given the situation, and so, after I'd asked my question—were the crenellations the problem?—I simply fell silent.

I remember she had to move her chair back from the table in order to get further away from me (she said something like *I can't sit here anymore*, though she didn't, as I recall, get up out of the chair), and something about the suddenness and violence of her movement brought my mind back into focus, drawing me, I mean, away from my obsessive and repetitive thinking about the feeling of doom, and, in that moment, I realized, first, that I had been having this conversation in the first place, and, second, that the conversation was serious and not something I could just walk away from or get out of having until I felt more myself. She was, I remember, accusing me of focusing too much on trivial things, like what to call the edges of the bowl we'd ended up agreeing wouldn't work for us, but really, I understood, given the vehemence with which she was now speaking, she was also telling me there were things I did and had done that she could not or simply would not any longer ignore or abide. I often found myself spending probably unhealthy amounts of time wondering what my wife was thinking, wondering, specifically, whether her outward actions were true signs of her feelings towards me or only the results of momentary impulses, or, worse, manifestations of a facade she'd put on, so my silence in that moment really didn't come out of a lack of consideration for her feelings or her way of thinking, and it also didn't come out of any inherent inability to consider her thoughts and feelings, but really and only out of, I think, a deep—and, I hope, sincere—respect for her and her native capacity to tell her own story better than I possibly could, by which I mean to explain why I'm not reporting any of the words she then said (though I know that this, too, will seem deceitful, still, I think it would be worse to misrepresent her than to simply say I didn't then and don't now know, not with any true understanding, what she was thinking or how she was feeling, and, in my state of mind, feeling doomed, I could think only of the story of the Judgment of Solomon, though I decided that telling it in that moment and to my wife, of all people, would only make the situation much, much worse, and, as she spoke, I could feel myself becoming more and more disappointed in my silence, more and more disgusted with myself, and, although I didn't want to do it because I didn't want to be accused of being manipulative, I couldn't help it, I began to cry, and I know I was thinking of the accident and imagining that what she was saying was in reference to the accident, even though I'm sure that, if asked, she would have said it had nothing to do with the accident—a topic she wouldn't bring up in any case, no matter how obviously it was the thing we were trying to talk about—and everything to do with the way I'd always treated her, always treated everyone, including our son, and which way of treating others was the reason she sometimes couldn't stand to be around me.

I was and continued to be silent, though now I was also weeping, and I knew my wife didn't like these *moods*, as she called them, and had told me as much, several times—it wasn't the first time I'd been distracted by some feeling or inner state that had taken up residence in me and which feeling or inner state then more or less completely overtook me—even, for a time, in concert with the social worker, encouraging me to see a therapist on my own. I wasn't, as I remember it, opposed to the idea, but she'd made this suggestion in a peculiarly aggressive way—*You need to figure your shit out*, I remembered she'd told me, which was strange for her (the aggression, I mean), so much so that even she recognized it, changing the subject altogether immediately after saying this—and, because I'd felt her suggestion was less a suggestion than an attack, I had, at the time, simply ignored it, and, after a while, this idea had disappeared from our conversations. This was, I now see, almost directly after I'd finally given up on my speech-acts-language project, and I could now see that, because there was so much I *couldn't* say, I probably had been difficult to get along with then, but of course, at the time, I didn't see this, probably *couldn't* have seen it. It was not a thought the speech-acts-language would allow, and even after I'd given up on the speech-acts-language, I'd been adamant that my thoughts as such were not *moods*, could not be moods, but still the end result of her referring so often to my *moods* was that I became less certain that my thoughts weren't in fact *the result* of my moods, which led me to wonder what *moods* were anyway, and whether they weren't in some way coterminal with thoughts, or else were maybe collections of individual thoughts constrained by time rather than by subject. A mood, I remember thinking, might not be a train of thought, maybe wasn't anything quite so linear, but might instead be a cloud or a swarm of perceptions and observations all occurring at roughly the same time. I chose not to share this thought with my wife, though I worried I'd only been set upon this particular train of thought through her use of the word, and then my natural indecision and intransigence eventually conquered her recommendations anyway, and the subject was, for a time between us, dropped.

On

Luis and Walter Alvarez and Comets

A night or two before the eclipse, I passed my wife watching something on her phone in bed, something very quiet but with the occasional word I could hear from where I'd stood in the bathroom about, I think, infants or young children and *the roles of the partner and the parent* (I remember that particular phrase because it was repeated, and because the definite article sounded so awkward to me in that context), I walked down the hallway through the living room and passed through the patio doors outside and over the short stretch of sandy lawn to the garage, where I tucked my son in and told him the story of Luis and Walter Alvarez and the so-called Alvarez Impact. I guess what I should really say, because I had little grasp of the science behind the Alvarezes' ideas and no interest in learning that science, is that I was telling him the story of the *reception* of the Alvarezes' hypothesis, which is to say that I was telling him the story of how frustrating it must have been for the Alvarezes to have this idea, an idea they must have thought would prove useful in extending the knowledge mankind as a whole possessed, an idea that might, very possibly, meet some small resistance at first but would, I told my son Luis Alvarez must have felt certain, eventually reach those who needed to hear it, those who could then build on it and move the rest of us forward, and whose ideas would, in retrospect, validate this idea, until even those who'd reacted poorly at first would come around. I told him, I mean, about the frustrations of having such an idea insulted by people who, I felt, in their criticism of that idea, were actually really only saying—this is what I told my son—*Look, I have a job*

I want to hang onto so that I can pay my mortgage, so that I can send my kids to college, so that I and my husband or wife don't go hungry (so that, ultimately, I have something to do with my time, preferably something that doesn't make me wish I had less of that time), and maybe if I keep on pretending to believe in this sham that people have forced me to pretend to believe in long enough, I can die before it's revealed to have been a sham all along, and I won't have to face up to my part in it, and because of all that, I have to say, cannot *say otherwise, that your idea, Alvarez, is just flat wrong and that you—a* physicist *of all things, not a paleontologist or even a geologist—are so thoroughly mistaken that even to call you a dilettante or a fool or completely out of your depth wouldn't be strong enough condemnation for this ridiculous idea you've published under your name* and your son's, *this shameful idea that you claim to have had.*

I'm not certain that any of what I'd said would have made sense to my son—I knew he would have been more interested in the dinosaurs that had supposedly been killed off by the effects of the impact than in how the Alvarezes' ideas about that impact were received by their fellow scientists, and anyway, the mosquitoes and the cicadas were getting to me; there's a limit to how long anyone or anything can put up with that noise in their ear. When he'd been alive, there had been no better way to get him to go to sleep than to sit and tell him about some train of thought I'd followed earlier in the day, even if, in this case, it was a train of thought I'd had several weeks before, at the time of the shooting, and that I was only now telling him about because I'd just finished his room the day before, and so this was my first chance to tell all of it to him. When I tried to tell my wife about these things—and this happened almost never now, but there had been a time, before our son was born, when I'd shared these thoughts with her— she would sometimes become angry, but mostly she just became sleepy—though now that I think of it, I wonder whether both my son and my wife had only pretended to be sleepy simply to stop me from talking. In the case of my son, it was always pretty much the same, whether he was sleeping or just pretending to sleep, because it almost never happened that, when he was pretending to sleep, he didn't then also actually fall asleep. (My son, at least, unlike my wife, usually also tried very hard to understand what I was saying; I remember the look on his face, a very serious look of concentration, as though, even though he didn't understand what I was saying, he still understood that it was something that was important to try to understand, and I always found this, this intense look of concentration, heartbreaking; it felt almost like I was keeping a secret from him.)

I remember that night I was telling him this story about Luis Alvarez and his son Walter Alvarez without even necessarily wanting to, but maybe as a way to force myself to think about something else, and, looking back on that moment, I can see how little interest any of what I was saying would have held for my son or for any child of his age, and thinking about the look he'd always had in these moments makes me feel almost cruel in retrospect. Something about what I was saying about Alvarez reminded me of the movie *Night of the Comet*, of especially the opening voiceover, and while I was trying to remember what it was that had saved the teenagers in the movie who'd been saved—it was that they'd all stayed the night in containers made of steel, I eventually remembered, and the strangeness of that, the staying in containers made of steel, is, I think, what made it stick in memory—I thought, finally, about the dinosaurs; as though lightning had flashed inside my mind, I remember I imagined a pair of brontosaurs, one very young, drawing their last breaths and expiring. I didn't envision *all* of the dinosaurs dropping dead at once and in a single instant—that, I knew, was a children's story, a fantasy hatched by those lacking imagination—but instead I saw these two, and others like them, dying from starvation or thirst or cold or wounds or all of those conditions together, much more pitifully and humbly than being struck by the asteroid and crushed or covered in lava or thrown into the air by an earthquake or drowned in a tidal wave. This wasn't sad to me, at least, not at the time—no, because of the context, I thought only of the obvious parallel between these dinosaurs and the scientists who had insulted the Alvarezes and of course the scientists in the movie, in *Night of the Comet*, who had somehow known to go into a bunker made of steel but who hadn't realized they'd meanwhile left the vents to the outside open, and who were, because of their oversight, during the course of the movie, slowly turning into zombies, battling the same strange extraterrestrial wasting disease every other human being had already succumbed to through regular transfusions of blood from people like the teenagers and even younger children who had managed to completely escape exposure to the comet and its gases. These scientists, I thought, must have thought that they were doing something valiant and altruistic, looking for the cure to this strange disease. No one else then alive, these scientists must have thought, I told my son, could do the work they were doing, and so, even though it must have been horrible for even these scientists, at least at first, to be murdering young children in order to stay alive (and here I remember I choked up and found it difficult to finish my sentence), they could only have believed that they *had* to do it, if only so that they themselves could stay alive to then do the research necessary to find the cure, so that, in turn, other young children could someday be born, and the arrogance of this—this belief that only *these* scientists could solve the problem, and the certainty that they *would* solve the problem—was so alien to me that it seemed almost the most fantastical part of the movie, more unlikely even than a comet streaking across the sky and turning most of humankind into a fine red dust that could then be washed away by the lightest drizzle of rain, and more unlikely than the idea that, among the survivors, most would be turned into zombies. These scientists, I told my son, could only have believed they could cure the disease but they had in fact, and in almost no time at all, discovered instead a new and more morally reprehensible way of killing off humanity, even their own humanity. At some point, I realized I shouldn't be telling my son any of this and so I stopped talking.

I saw then that my son's arm, dangling over the edge of the

bed, had an unnatural bend in it at the shoulder, as though the point at which the arm met the shoulder sat below the socket I'd made with the rubber band and the T-shirt, his arm looking, in other words, like it might fall off, and so, while I tried to get back on track in what I'd been saying, to, I think, explain about the Chicxulub crater, I reached over, grabbed the boy's arm, and tested it, slowly, gently pulling his arm back into place. I'd been worried about this earlier, about, I guess, the suitability of this particular toy—a wrestler, I thought, or some hero or villain whose profession or secret identity required that he wear scant clothing made out of what looked like Spandex (a dancer? an Olympic athlete?) and who had hands that could be manipulated into a variety of grips (this is what had, I thought, suggested the toy's use as an arm, or really, as a hand, in the first place). I'd worried about the socket I'd made to attach it, about whether that socket would keep the wrestler toy in place, and now I could see it hadn't.

I had, I remember, chosen this toy, this clumsy, oversized rubber- or plastic-and-polyester *action figure*, because it had been one of his favorites, but now I wondered whether he hadn't been attached to it primarily because of where and when he'd acquired it—it was something we bought him while on the trip to see my wife's mother, the kind of trip I could just remember being bored by when I was myself the child in the backseat (though our son was still much too young to be forming memories, I thought—I didn't remember anything at all from when I was his age; the car trips I was thinking about would have been a few years in his future (and even this thought was enough to make me want to weep)), and I suddenly remembered a fight we'd had on that trip, my wife and I, about whether we ought to stop for gas (my wife, sitting in the passenger seat, said that we would run out of gas and wouldn't be able to find a gas station if we kept going—was I going to walk to the next exit if that happened? what about her? what about the boy? were they just going to sit there, in the hot car? it was too hot for that—while I, sitting in the driver's seat, directly in front of the gauge, visibly at a quarter of a tank, told her it would be fine, we would make it to the next station just fine, to which she answered that I always contradicted her, even on things that were perfectly obvious, like how much gas we had), and I wondered about how it could have been to be my son, to be in his position at such moments, seeing and hearing what he'd seen and heard. After we'd stopped and everyone had calmed down a little, I'd taken him into the gas station to change his diaper and to see if there was anything there to distract him from what had become a kind of shared distress—hearing his mother upset had, naturally, made him upset—and there was this toy, a cheap toy that I guessed he wouldn't have given a second thought to in a store full of toys, but seen here, in a place where there were really no other toys, it stuck out, and I remembered also that, within a few miles and from what I could see in the rearview mirror, it seemed as though he'd already created a whole world in his car seat, a whole world all to himself and this wrestler, who my son called Barry, I think I remember—and I worried even then that I'd misunderstood its importance to him, because what if the toy I was thinking of was one of any number of other toys he'd had at that time, and this one, the wrestler, had been a toy he'd never really played with except on that car trip, a toy he'd only played with afterwards to humor me because I'd bought it for him at a particularly low moment, thinking it was, in some ways, like the toys he liked and so not obviously inferior, but that in fact he liked *those* toys for inscrutable reasons, reasons, that is to say, that were inscrutable to me but perfectly comprehensible to him, reasons that made *this* toy, the one I had in my hand now, one of his *least* favorites? What if, I wondered, he'd played with one of the toys my wife had thrown away much more often when I wasn't around, and, thinking of or hoping for that toy, I'd instead mistakenly saved this one? Maybe, I thought, this was the reason that, despite the careful work I'd put into the socket, the arm wouldn't stay put.

He Describes a Dream

I remember I awoke the next morning having suffered a kind of anxiety attack in the middle of the night and, as a result, I remember I felt unrested and really not up to fixing my son's arm or even going out to the garage at all although I had nothing else to do that day. There were often nights like this one, where I would wake from a somewhat lucid dream into an unstoppable flow of thoughts, as though I had not only been long awake but had even been deeply engaged in the most strenuous mental processes, but I could never understand exactly what it was, in my dreams, that provoked these torrents of thoughts, mostly because I only seldom remembered anything about those dreams—the anxiety attack that followed tended to obliterate all traces of them, and, when I thought about my seemingly sleepless night later, I couldn't remember the dream I'd had while sleeping, but instead remembered only the horrible stretch of consciousness that followed, in which I tossed and turned or simply worried, unable to go back to sleep or to get up, and thus could only wonder if there might have been a connection between what I'd dreamt and what I'd thought about upon waking.

But then maybe this night wasn't so much like those other nights after all, because even now I can remember most of the elements of the dream I had, and I even remember those elements better than the train of thought that followed the dream (though, because these trains of thought tended to be mostly single-minded and their concerns more or less universal even when their particular anxieties were tied to recent events, I have anyway a fairly good idea of what kinds of thoughts I must have had while lying awake—my wife, her appointment with the lawyer that I'd found in her calendar—despite not having any clear idea of what *specific* thoughts I had while lying awake that *particular* night or early morning). That night, I dreamed about a dragon—this was the only word that came to mind to describe the creature in the dream, though the actual creature in the dream had been, as far as I could remember, pretty small, the size and even the general shape of a dachshund—hiding or, more properly, living in the bole of a tree. I dreamed that I had come much too close to this tree after being warned not to get too close to it—and this was one of those experiences where dread really comes in, where you know you're doing something you've been warned never to do, but, in the dream, you feel powerless not to do it—and I'd been bitten, as I thought of it, even though I think in the dream this dragon had never so much as touched me, much less bit me. Instead, somehow, through some method I'm not sure I ever even attempted to understand, not in the dream, the dragon had infected me with something called *The Great Decline*, which began, in the dream, with my head, where my hair melted onto my scalp until it looked like a flat, plastic wig. This *Decline* then proceeded down, over my chest and back, all the way to my toes, slowly and with different effects depending on the part of the body it affected. Though I say now that it had different effects on each part of the body, I don't remember specifically what any of these effects were—melting or warping and distending, but not which part had been melted and which distended—only that the end result was that I looked unformed or unreal in some strange way, as though my body had been sculpted from clay but then abandoned by its maker before any real detail work had been done, kind of like a poorly made mannequin, I guess. This *Decline* was also somehow infectious, and I could, I found, transmit it to others by saying some specific word—not, I think, a word that was archaic or unusual but also not one that would normally have come up in conversation, a word I really can't remember, unfortunately, but a word which, in the dream, and in the situations in which I found myself in the dream, somehow kept coming up. I mean that I would find myself—horrified at my appearance and my general state—in conversation with another person, another person who, I should say, I very much wanted to guard against the possible infection with and detrimental effects of this *Decline*, but then the conversation would get to a point where it could only proceed after I'd said this word aloud, either because the person seemed in some way to be encouraging me to say the word, even antagonizing me or bullying me into saying it, or else because we'd had some basic misunderstanding that could only be cleared up through my use of the word. In the cases in which the person seemed to be forcing me to say the word, I remember, there was a point at which I felt, in a strange way, relieved to finally say it, as though I were getting revenge on them, a revenge I hadn't, I think, not really, not at first, wanted to take, but which, as the conversation went on, came to seem more and more necessary, and I think, in the dream, that I'd felt some kind of relief or even triumph, despite my guilt over what I knew would happen to the person.

I think maybe that makes it sound like I infected lots of people in the dream, and, in the dream, I remember, it felt as though I were running from one person to another, infecting each one, helpless to stop the process and disgusted by my actions, but, thinking about it afterwards, I realized there couldn't have been that many infections, not really, because after all, I woke fairly soon after falling asleep, perhaps an hour or two after getting into bed, and I'm certain, at least, of what time it was when I awoke. I can remember looking at the clock and then, despite the hour, getting up. Still, while I was asleep, it seemed as though the incident with the dragon and even my own *Decline* had taken up relatively little time in the dream, and so the dream had mostly been this process of meeting a person, feeling terrified that I would infect him or her or them with the *Decline*, and then, because of how that person acted and spoke, being *forced* into infecting them. I can't remember how the dream ended.

Naturally, I didn't mention any of this to my wife, though she asked me why I hadn't slept and told me my absence from the bed—and my tossing and turning before I'd gotten up—had kept her awake. Though she must have felt as exhausted as I did, still, she was, in that moment and for that moment only, caring and thoughtful and concerned less with her own state of well-being than she was with mine, and this was a little surprising at the time because, well, there was her appointment later that day, about which we still hadn't spoken. In the moment, I remember, I wondered that she could be both a person who lost her patience in an instant over something others wouldn't have even noticed, and one who also thought nothing of crouching in front of a snarling stray dog to read the number off its collar so that she could call its owner to say she'd found it—all of this during the first bands of a tropical storm—and, when there was no answer, keep calling until she got through, and even seem surprised when the person on the other end of the call finally picked up and acknowledged that, yes, the dog was theirs but, well, there was a storm, they couldn't come now, and so, because the dog wouldn't come home with her, she'd stayed there in the corner of the yard with the dog, getting soaked, and I was truly ashamed of myself that I simply wasn't capable of that kind of generosity or fellow feeling.

That morning, though, the morning after the dream, while I was standing at the sink making coffee, she asked about my night and I told her I hadn't noticed anything out of the ordinary—and, strictly speaking, aside from the fact of my remembering the dream and getting out of bed in the middle of the night, this was after all only the truth: I'd sat at the kitchen table in the dark, thinking obsessively about something I'd come to think of as *the matter*, the thing we couldn't speak about with each other, even though *the matter* was a thing we would, eventually and probably very soon, *have* to speak about with each other, but which, because we were, at that point, not really speaking at all, about anything, *the matter* was just yet another thing we weren't speaking about. In answering this way, I didn't—I want to be clear—intend to dismiss her; I hoped, by answering that nothing much had happened, I would also be assuring her and through her myself, that there was really nothing in what had happened the night before worth discussing further, nothing, that is, with which she needed to concern herself. Because that day was a day on which, I knew, there were things she needed to do, things that required some degree of concentration and planning—and there was, at that time, always also *the matter* (*to be dealt with later* was the way I think we both thought of it at the time, or at least the way we both seemed to treat it) that we were both trying not to mention or think about, and that only seemed to come up in our conversation as a result of something unrelated and seemingly innocuous, like this dream I'd had, or her insistence on knowing what it was that had kept me up—I wanted only, I think, to help her not think about me or my sleeplessness, though this came out as silence and probably only made the problem worse. Given the particular matter we were trying not to address, I later thought, and given our usual pattern—me trying to move the conversation to another topic; her frustration with my seeming refusal to answer her directly—I probably should have just told her about my dream, even though I am and always have been of the opinion that there's really nothing so boring or more likely to later be looked upon as a complete and utter waste of time as telling someone about a dream or hearing someone tell you about their dream. I was certain she knew this about me (she did sometimes start to tell me about her dreams before, inevitably and probably rudely, I tried to change the topic by asking a question unrelated to what she was saying or by announcing there was something that needed to be done in another part of the house) and would remember that, even if I'd had a dream I remembered—which would, as I'm sure she *did* know, be unusual for me—I still wouldn't tell her about it, wouldn't think the dream I'd had would be noteworthy or important enough to share, and wouldn't want to bore her by telling her about it, ultimately, against her wishes, even if she'd explicitly asked me to, mainly because the dream would be as incomprehensible and insignificant to her as her dreams were to me, but now I realize she was probably really only asking for some relief from her own anxieties and worries, especially those about the particular matter that, I'm sure we both realized, we would have to take care of later, and I now realize also that I could easily have provided this relief, would have been willing to do so, had I known the eventual outcome, willing to encourage her to laugh at me and the dream's fantastical worries, and that I had, then, failed twice over, first, by keeping her awake—though I strongly suspected it wasn't my restlessness that had kept her awake, or not my restlessness by itself—and then, through refusing her this mindless but diverting bit of conversation in the kitchen (and we still, weeks after the break-ins had ended and the suicide had taken place, were avoiding the living room, and especially the couch). I poured the coffee and sat down at the counter instead of the table, where my wife was sitting. The strained silence extended until I didn't feel that anything I could do, not even relenting and telling her about the dream, would end it, and so I got up, I remember, leaving my cup still half full, and told her I needed to take a shower.

His Son's Room

I remember I passed my son's room, by this time empty apart from the two moving boxes on the lowest shelf above where his bed had been, and wondered, again, how we'd ever fit so much stuff into the space. Before, with his things in it, I'd often felt much too large to be inside of this room, and so, during the day, I'd rarely entered it, and only when necessary; once inside, I inevitably found myself feeling the same sensation I'd felt the time I'd gone to his daycare before pick-up time (my wife had been out of town and I'd had class at his normal pick-up time and had had to bring him to class with me): a constant, low-level fear I was, without realizing it, standing on something very important, or else was about to step on something extremely delicate and fragile, a worry that was heightened by concern that, if I moved my feet at all to check whether I was, in fact, standing on something I shouldn't have been, I would in the process crush something even more vital, something, I mean, living. Even in the hallway outside of the room where all the children were, I'd wanted, I remembered, to somehow float above the floor, or else to shrink myself to an appropriate size, and I recalled feeling that all of the tiny beings in the next room were completely blind to the danger they were in, but the woman who ran the daycare, as I remember her, had been on edge, ultra-vigilant—not *hovering*, no, because the room was much too small for such a thing, and because it must have been obvious to her that to do so would really be only to make the whole problem worse, but *watching*—not passively, as in *watching television* but actively, as in *night watchman*; in other words, observing me closely, anticipating my moves before I'd moved, before I'd done anything at all, and I knew this wasn't simply because I'd arrived early (though, given the way she was watching me, I did wonder whether my wife had in fact called before she'd left town to let the woman know about me picking up our son early that day) but that she was showing me that she was ready at the slightest hint of a problem to jump in front of the children, or at least, if she couldn't get in the way, to shriek at me to move my left foot, to watch where I was stepping, to be more careful, as though it were possible to be more careful than I then felt I ought to be.

No, more often, when the boy was in his room, instead of going in, I just looked at him from where I stood, on the other side of the doorframe in our bedroom, out of, in other words, crushing distance of his fingers and toys, as though I were observing a very small animal in its enclosure at the zoo through the thick glass (or was it plastic? in my mind, it was a very thick, heavily scratched and slightly greasy clear something that might have been either plastic or glass) aperture. I hadn't felt like this when he was a newborn, picking him up and swooping him through the air in front of me at arms' length, handing him over to my wife without even bothering to cradle his head, with only the tips of my fingers supporting his neck and all of his limbs flailing, but after he started moving around on his own I began to worry, all the time, that he was in danger, specifically from me. In fact I felt, sometimes, often, that it might have been better for him had he been, for that time in his life, behind glass, or else that *I* had been behind glass, that it would have been better, I mean, that we had been in some way separated, physically separated, from each other. I didn't go into his room to clean or even to pick up, not because I had some chauvinistic idea that these actions weren't, somehow, *my role* but because, once I'd entered the room, I would worry—unreasonably, I know—that there would then be no room for my son, no room for him to move around once he'd entered, no room for him to leave if he then wanted to. Though it was really only *nearly* the case, I felt as though the boy's room were only slightly bigger than my body, and that once I'd entered the room, there was really no space for anything else. I very nearly only ever went in if he was already in bed and I knew there would be room for me, only went in, I mean, either to tuck him in or after he'd already fallen asleep, and only very occasionally during the day, to get a toy or a shirt or a coat for him, and, on those brief and infrequent daytime visits, I always told him to stay outside of the room until I'd finished, even though I knew this probably scared him.

The boy's room, I should probably explain, had been a large-ish walk-in closet when we first moved into the house, and we'd made a plan to move to a bigger house or apartment after we'd found out my wife was pregnant, a place where we'd all have our own rooms, even my wife and I—it'd been clear even then that such an arrangement would help matters between us, though we hadn't wanted to say as much and had just talked about her having her *own space*, a place for her to relax; she had, I remember, even picked out a loveseat she wanted to put in this space, though, when the boy was born, we'd been flat broke, unable to pay even the hospital bill—and a place where all of the rooms would *be* rooms, not walk-in closets, but then we hadn't moved, for several reasons, not the least of which was, in fact, our son, who was born almost a month premature and then of course there was also the storm, which had cut down to almost nothing the number of available rentals. When it had been just his crib and him—and, of course, the innumerable gadgets and toys and necessities my wife and her father and stepmother had insisted he *must* have—the room had seemed adequate, more or less (my wife and I fought about how much stuff she wanted to fit in there), and, because it was next to our bedroom, it was in fact a perfectly convenient situation; it was a room that really wasn't a room but that had a door, so we could, in time, begin the long, very long process of acclimating him to sleeping alone, in his own room. But then, when he'd outgrown his crib and needed a toddler bed, and really even before this, when, as he seemed to get bigger and bigger every day and had obviously outgrown his crib, his room had seemed to shrink, like his clothes seemed to, my wife and I talked about moving again, even though, again, we didn't get around to it.

In our son's room, this former walk-in closet, there had been the bed and a bit of floor next to the bed where he sometimes played, maybe the size of the bed or maybe just slightly narrower (and this was the part of the room I thought of as, roughly, me-sized), and also a small dresser where we kept all of his clothes—really, nothing more could comfortably fit in the room, but, still, there were moments when I looked in from outside the room, when he was there, on the floor, playing, when everything seemed more or less according to scale, like an optical illusion that lost its power as soon as he pulled himself up or made a move toward me. The room had been, long before we'd moved in, I think, a very short hallway leading from the mud room to the bedroom, a hallway that had, when the house was divided into apartments, been retrofitted with a set of two long, heavy shelves high up on the interior wall, and, underneath them, a long bar for hanging clothes had been installed. The room had a window opposite the bar, which seemed strange, both for a hallway and (even more so) for a closet, but there were many things about the house that were strange, some of them due to the dividing—our bathroom had no windows, for instance—and others no doubt due simply to the age of the house, to the date of its original construction, when, I guessed, people's needs were different or their expectations were different, and when, I'd always been told, people were, on average, smaller and shorter, taking up less space, all of which explained the relatively (especially for the neighborhood) cheap rent.

When he'd outgrown the crib, we'd tried to make some small changes to make it seem more like a room: We'd removed the clothes bar before jamming the toddler bed in lengthwise at the far end of the room and blocking what had been the door to the mudroom with the dresser, giving him some privacy and giving me and my wife a place to put at least some of his many toys and books and clothes. I tried putting the dresser under (really, in front of) the window—this gave him the most space to play,

I pointed out—but my wife worried that the shelves we couldn't remove might somehow come loose from their brackets and crash down on him. (Needless to say, his bed still had to go under these shelves; there was no other place for it in the room, but my wife seemed to think that putting the dresser under the shelves, too, made the room safe enough to be acceptable.) In order to accommodate all of his toys, especially the bigger stuffed animals and anything that wouldn't fit in the drawers of the dresser, behind his bed, we had to put them in bright fabric-covered cardboard boxes with animal faces on them, foxes and raccoons and bears, up on the high shelves, even though this naturally meant that he couldn't get them down himself, and even though we knew, I think, that the shelves themselves would become a serious temptation for him as something to climb, most especially at just the moments when we weren't around to monitor him, when he was supposed to be playing or napping in his room alone, which is to say most especially when it was most dangerous for him. Fortunately, though, the dresser was relatively short and the bed was a low-slung racing car, nearly touching the floor, so there was nothing in his room tall enough that, at his height, he would have been able to climb up to the shelves—only my wife and I could reach them, and I needed a footstool to reach the highest shelf—but then, in a way, the whole arrangement must have seemed needlessly cruel, since we'd effectively put all of his things in view but so high up that he couldn't possibly ever reach them. My wife and I assured each other it was temporary, we'd find a bigger, better place to live, but then it hadn't been temporary, though I don't want to imply that its effective permanence was in any way her fault, not any more than it was my fault. The situation wasn't intended to be permanent, is what I mean to say, and that it turned out to last longer than it should have was really only fate playing itself out.

In Which

He Explains About the Hair Dryer

It wasn't a surprise that we would—that we did—drag our feet about even going to the Macy's to look for a replacement decorative bowl in the first place, or that, once we found ourselves in the Macy's, we didn't immediately go to the HOME section to look for the replacement bowl we'd already seen online, the bowl I knew exactly where to find, since the website had informed me that that particular bowl was in stock at this particular Macy's, and was located in the HOME section on floor three. In theory, this was a trip—to the Macy's, I mean—that either my wife or I could have made alone (we might even have simply ordered the bowl online and had it delivered to us at home, though, because of the strikes (safety, it was said; drivers were routinely killed on their routes now), if we'd done so, it would have taken three to four weeks to arrive (the Macy's was two miles away, and we could pick it up that day if we chose that option)), but I think none of this occurred to us at the time because we were both, frankly, afraid to make the trip at all, much less alone. What I guess I'm trying to say is that we were both well aware that the bowl that had broken was the one *our son* had broken, the bowl he'd broken while playing in the front room, alone, while I worked in the bedroom, as I usually did on days when I watched him all day or in the mornings before I dropped him off at daycare, the bowl he'd broken while my wife was at work, and, because I was on my own, answering student emails while also trying to get through a draft of a paper on the language the Man of the Hole spoke that I planned to present at a conference the following week—it was office hours, at least

technically, even though I wasn't on campus, and so I couldn't simply ignore the emails (one student was sick, another had been sick,
one thought she was getting sick, several students were turning
in papers that had been due weeks before because they had been
sick, there were questions about the assignment due next week, my
book order for the fall was overdue, did I want to teach this summer?), and so I made the decision to put my son in the bathtub
with just enough water at the bottom that he couldn't drown; he
had ceramic chips all over him, in his hair, even in his eyelashes,
and I was worried he would be covered in tiny cuts if I tried to
brush them off with my hands or the washrag we usually used
when giving him a bath, and my plan, I remember, was to pour
water over him with a plastic cup from the kitchen, which is what
I'd seen my wife doing when he'd been an infant—while I went
back into the front room to quickly clean up most of the mess
he'd made and grab the cup from the kitchen, so that when the
lights blinked off and I heard that horrible, loud thump coming,
I thought, from the back of the house, I really had no idea what it
could be, but I was very worried that it had been my son.

My wife left late for work that morning, I remember, partly
in order to show me, contrary to what had been said during our
argument the night before, that her schedule was at least flexible
enough to give her the time to take our son to daycare twice a
week, so it wasn't true that I had to drop him off every single day,
even on those days I taught (which, because his daycare wasn't
close by but was on the way to campus, in turn meant I dropped
him off long past the usual drop-off time on such days so that I
didn't spend my morning driving back and forth and could instead spend the morning getting ready for the rest of the day—the
woman there had complained to me, several times, about this, and
I wondered aloud to my wife whether this woman resented our
son and treated him differently as a result, and I was sorry that we
were putting him in such a difficult position—and that I would
often be late for my office hours (unless I held them at home, from
my laptop, on those days I wasn't teaching, although doing this

inevitably meant that a student would then show up in person to my office on campus, a thing that never happened when I was on campus), which in turn led to my annual evaluations showing somewhat lower scores, which in turn led to my *ranking* at the end of the year making it difficult, so she said, for the chair to justi-fy keeping me on—frankly, I'd always relied on the department's disorganization for my continued employment, I knew; had they been better organized, I was certain I would have been replaced much earlier, but as it was, they could barely keep up with replac-ing the departing tenure-track professors). At the real heart of this argument, I suspected, was my wife's belief that I didn't respect what she did, though I'd often tried to explain that this couldn't be further from the truth—that, despite the fact that it paid poorly, even worse than my own job, I had nothing but respect for what she did—and that it was only that my own work required a great deal of time *not* spent in class, i.e., research time, that, as I'd said over and over, I was nevertheless never paid for and that therefore seemed (even to me, on occasion) like something I did merely for fun or as a hobby, like, for example, the paper I was planning on presenting about the language the Man of the Hole spoke, but which research was in fact the sole reason I'd been hired in the first place, and would, besides, be my only chance to move up in the academic world. By all of which I simply mean that she saw my schedule, seemingly wide open, and had made her decisions about child care accordingly; I could do this, I could do that. Her job was eight to five, Monday through Friday, which meant that she really couldn't spare the time to pick up our son or drop him off. She *could* get up early; it *was* possible—because she couldn't always pick him up in the afternoon, we'd agreed, when starting daycare, that she would drop him off some mornings—but inevitably in-stead she'd get up late, complaining about her headache or of not sleeping well or both, and she would be in a rush, or else (and this was intensely frustrating) she would just *act* like she was in a rush, and she would get angry with me when I reminded her that this was one of the days when she was supposed to drop him off—*I*

have to get to work, she'd say, implying that, because my classes
didn't start for another hour and a half, I had nothing but time to
drop him off, when the fact was I still hadn't finished the lecture
I'd be giving that morning and I hadn't graded any of the essays
that had been turned in the previous week (because of course we
had to go to the zoo on the weekend, we couldn't possibly just stay
home, and if I couldn't go with them, well, that was too bad, and
I felt guilty and worried about missing something, and so I went,
and then none of the work I'd needed to do was done), and, really,
she rarely got up early anymore (she believed she wasn't a *morning person*, and would show me articles supposedly explaining that
people who *naturally* woke up later were more creative and more
empathetic and that so-called *morning people* who looked down on
late risers as lazy (I'd never accused my wife of being lazy, though,
on occasion, I did come just up to the edge of thinking it) couldn't
be more wrong, as though there were some set of traits that everyone who *naturally* woke up after nine o'clock shared, traits all
those who, like me, rose early (partly because there were these in-
furiating people who refused to wake up at reasonable times, and
someone had to make breakfast, *someone* had to get our son ready
for daycare, *someone* had to drop him off there, too) did not and,
apparently constitutionally, could not possess). Anyway, although
she'd woken up early—she set her alarm the night before, and I
was convinced she'd waited until I'd finished brushing my teeth
and had come to bed to set the alarm, so that I could watch her
set her alarm—she'd then spent thirty minutes showing me how
slowly she moved when she woke up too early, emphasizing, with
each thing she did, how tired she still was, how bad she felt without sleep, until finally she had not only passed the time she should
have left if she was going to drop our son off at daycare, she had
even passed the time she normally left for work (and I knew later
this would be used as part of her argument against waking up early,
as though somehow giving herself extra time in the morning had
actually caused her to have less time in the end; she would never
see this as ridiculous, of course, and would become angry with me

if I pointed out how silly it was as an argument), and then, in her haste to show that she was now in a rush to leave, she left her hair dryer plugged in on the vanity, with the cord dangling off the edge in a loop near the floor.

Later, much later, my wife would say that, had the ambulance only arrived earlier, meaning—in fact, coming almost to the point of saying—that, had 911 been called earlier, there might have been a chance, even though it was clear this was not the case. This was the thing that she said most often after the accident, that there might have been a chance. If the doctor hadn't argued with her about the things she told the doctor to do, there might have been a chance. If I hadn't argued with her that the doctor ought to know what to do in this situation—much better than we did, I mean, considering all of her training and her experience and our lack of those things—my wife might have gotten her way and there might have been a chance. And, thinking about it now, I can see that all of this was both a kind of wish fulfillment or fantasy and a way of trying to deal with the loss. I worry that the way I've explained it here makes it seem as though I take no responsibility for what happened, when, in fact, and at the time especially, I took *all* of the responsibility, which I realize now was a serious mistake, not only for me but also for my wife, who first reacted badly to this basically selfish act on my part and then, trying to take some agency back, finally accepted that version of events as the most accurate one and started blaming me for everything, not only for what the doctor told her was happening or what she'd seen happen, but even for things that simply hadn't occurred.

That day, it was only a transformer that had blown, not even the first one that had blown that month, but I had, after I realized my son wasn't making any noise whatsoever, maybe fifteen steps from the door of the bathroom, had the horrifying thought that he'd pulled on the hair dryer's cord, it had tumbled off the counter and into the bathtub, and he'd been electrocuted. I of course rushed into the bathroom, but there was a part of me that wanted only to turn around, run out through the door into the yard, and not ever go back. I was the one who'd put him in the bathtub and left him unsupervised. I was the one who hadn't bothered to make sure the hair dryer was unplugged, that it was far enough away from the bathtub that our son wouldn't reach for it and pull it into the tub. I was, as usual, the one who should take the blame, because I was the one without the presence of mind to know what should have been done. My impulse, in the moment, was to blame my wife for what I thought had happened, to say that she shouldn't have left the thing plugged in and on the edge of the vanity, and this was, of course, true—these were things that she shouldn't have done, and they were self-evidently things she shouldn't have done. But I also knew that this way of thinking was stupid—ultimately, it was my fault that I'd put our son in the tub with water in it and left him there by himself, with the hair dryer still plugged in and still precariously situated on the vanity. So many things could have gone wrong, with my son in the bathtub by himself, and my impulse to blame my wife for what I thought had happened wouldn't have prevented anything from happening; ultimately, I think, it would only really contribute to the poisoning of our relationship.

He Corrects the Record, or Attempts to Correct the Record

I worry that, in mentioning the hair dryer at all, I may have been trying to deflect blame for what really ended up happening, and, while it is true that my wife often left her hair dryer plugged in, next to the sink, even after getting so mad at me for putting the hair dryer in the sink that one time (which, as far as I can remember, I'd done only because the hair dryer, when I'd discovered it, had been lying on the floor, on the messy bathroom floor, and because, unlike my wife, I tended to use things and then put them away—my wife only did this when it suited her (which was rarely, and usually only ever in the run-up to an argument with me about putting things away so that she could say that she put things away and that my claims otherwise were exaggerated or simply wrong), and only tended to notice that things weren't put away if those things were in her way or else not where she'd put them, as with the hair dryer, in the sink rather than on the floor, where anyone could see it didn't belong, but for which placement she had some impossibly strained reason that of course involved some shortcoming for which I was ultimately to blame; it was *my* fault we hadn't rented a place with a vanity that was a reasonable size), it was also true that I'd told her that, if she was worried about electrocution— she claimed, later, to be worried about *my* electrocution, and *our son's* electrocution, though she'd begun criticizing me by saying that, if the hair dryer had gotten wet, *she* would have been electrocuted the next time she turned it on—if she was worried about electrocution, that maybe, instead of leaving the thing on the floor, plugged in, she could easily just unplug it and put it away (and this was an unwise thing to say, and, besides that, probably also an unnecessary thing to say, though at the time I'd thought, at least as I remember it, that it was a perfectly reasonable thing to say, maybe because I thought it would convince her I was right and my opinion wasn't, I said, even all that unusual (*most* people put their hair dryers away after they'd used them, because they knew the risks of leaving them out, still plugged in)), and that she'd then left the house without saying a word to me and hadn't come back until much later that evening, long after I'd realized how stupid I'd been and had called and left messages in her voicemail asking what she wanted to do for dinner (a transparent way to effect reconciliation, I thought, to show her I was contrite and would be willing to have a longer and more civil conversation if only she would please come home (meanwhile, our son was crying and wouldn't stop because I'd stepped on one of his toys and broken it and I didn't know what he usually did in the evenings because they were typically my only time to do real work, and so he was also off schedule, more or less completely, and probably needed to be fed and then put down, and I was desperate to have some kind of help, any kind of help)), anyway, while it is true that she left the hair dryer plugged in and in this precarious position, what really happened is that our son hadn't pulled on the cord and so the hair dryer hadn't fallen in the bathtub and the lights hadn't gone out because the hair dryer had fallen in the bathtub and our son hadn't been electrocuted. At the time of our argument about her leaving the hair dryer plugged in—which long predated the day our son broke the bowl—I remember thinking that she was probably just embarrassed to have been caught doing something irresponsible and even ultimately dangerous to people she professed to love, but still she continued to leave the hair dryer out, plugged in, long after we'd had this argument, including, as I've already said, the day our son broke the bowl and I'd had to leave him alone in the bathroom (in fact, she left the hair dryer plugged in and out on the counter or on the floor, or even, on more than a few occasions, on the back of the toilet (I didn't say anything about this after that one time, though I remember thinking, each time I noticed it, that this was a perfect example of her unreasonableness and her frankly hypocritical attitude to everything regarding our son and his safety—if *she* did it, or if it was *her* idea, it was the best way to do something; if *I* did it, or if it was in any way an idea that *I* had come up with, it was wrong and foolish, and possibly even dangerous, and this was an attitude that extended beyond our raising of our son and into other parts of our lives, too, and which attitude infuriated me)).

But on that day, I'd left our son in the bathtub and I'd started to clean up the bits of ceramic—I would later, much later, almost a year later, in fact, find still more of them in the carpet, deep in the fibers, when I shook the thing out, and this may have been part of what prompted me to say we ought to replace the bowl rather than find some other way to keep the sideboard clean (which suggestion of course then led to our trip to the Macy's)—and then, telling myself not to forget to get the cup from the kitchen, my phone buzzed, and I'd answered it even though I didn't recognize the number, probably only because I was flustered, and didn't think before swiping up on the phone's lockscreen, and, on the other end, it had been someone whispering hoarsely, I couldn't tell about what—maybe it was a foreign language?—but I remember hearing what I thought was a television playing *Law & Order* in the background, and for some reason this reminded me that I thought I'd seen my wife's hair dryer plugged in and on the counter in the bathroom earlier that morning (I mean, I guess, that I hadn't seen it when I'd brought my son to the bathtub; I'd been too preoccupied with his eyes—there was this dust in his hair and his eyelashes and I didn't want his eyes to get scratched or cut by the little bits of ceramic, especially since his hands kept going up to his face to clear away what was there) and then there was the thump and the lights went out and I'm sure I panicked.

Not that this was something the neighborhood had suffered from since we'd moved in—we'd had two or three years of living in the house with no problems whatsoever, other than tropical storms or hurricanes that came close but were never a direct hit—but the power outages had gotten so bad by then that both of our next-door neighbors had had very large (and very loud, really nearly deafening) generators installed and I feel like I must have heard those generators start up while sprint-walking through the house in just the light from the windows—there were, I remember, huge clouds blocking out the sun, and the day was very dark—over the sound of my son crying in the bathtub. The bathroom is an inside room (it was where we went when there were tornado warnings; we'd had several that year already) and it didn't have any windows, and I could hear our son going from crying, which he'd been do-ing since I'd set him down in the tub and left the bathroom, to gasping and screaming, although, in the circumstances, and given what, just a moment before, I'd been so terrified about, this sound was, frankly, a relief. It would be completely dark in there with no power and no lights, I realized, and so I put down the cup and grabbed the camping lantern we'd left out on the counter from the last tornado warning, clicked it on, cupped my shaking hands and poured water over his head a few times, and, trying to seem calm, took him out of the tub, dried him off, and put him in his bedroom while I finished cleaning up in the front room as best I could with only the lantern to help me find the glinting bits of the bowl on the floor.

When she got home, I remember, and because I'd spent that whole morning dealing with the broken bowl and the power out-age, I complained to my wife that I hadn't had time to work on the lecture I gave that day, which, in turn, meant that the class had been mostly recycled material from previous lectures that se-mester, and that it had ended forty-five minutes early, at which point everyone, including me, had been thoroughly confused, and I even thought, I told her, that I'd apologized to one or two stu-dents who'd stayed behind to ask about things I'd said that day. My wife, who, not unreasonably, probably didn't much care to hear my complaints the moment she walked in the door from a long day at work, said, *So, you want me to take him to daycare tomorrow, is that what you're saying? Why can't you just ask? Why is it so hard for you to just say: I want you to take him to daycare tomorrow?* In retrospect, I realize this was a perfectly appropriate response, given the long history of these complaints and the circumstances we, by then, were in, but at the time, I remember only that I reacted poorly, and wound up sleeping on the couch that night. My wife and I, if we spoke at all that night, spoke very little.

My wife, though, woke up late the next day—not unusual for her—and so she was in a hurry, because now, as she made a point of stopping what she was doing to tell me even though, as I'd pointed out before, stopping what she was doing meant she would be in even more of a hurry than if she had just gone on getting ready and getting our son ready (which I helped with, even though my wife took every opportunity to tell me what I was doing in order to help was wrong: *That shirt is dirty; he needs his other shoes; he doesn't like that kind of cheese; you know he's allergic to that*), now she had to drop off our son before getting to work, and she had a bunch of meetings today, the first was in just thirty minutes, and so she really couldn't afford to be late, all of which, her tone seemed to imply, were somehow my fault. In any case, because of the way she was acting—she would say because of my selfishness—neither one of us got to say much to our son that morning, and I worry now that we probably both treated him roughly in our haste to be rid of each other, so that when, barely an hour later, the sound of the bomb going off made me turn on the television to see if they were reporting anything about what had sounded like a very loud explosion and the footage they were showing was of the street where our son's daycare was—you could see the playground in the background of one shot, I remember—there was, for me, nothing but an intense anxiety and a hard, bitter regret.

He Describes a Bird or an Insect of Some Kind

About a month before I experienced that first feeling of doom, about a month, I mean, before I stood, staring at my wife's back, unable to decide whether to do anything to comfort her, in the aisle at the Macy's next to that embarrassing Easter display, I was sitting in front of the window in my office at the university, trying unsuccessfully, for what was, I think, the fourth or fifth day in a row, to bring myself finally to once and for all read and comment on a set of student papers, probably thinking, as I usually do, about my reluctance to actually read and grade them and the—proximate, not ultimate—reasons for that reluctance, since it isn't as though I didn't know I would be done reading and grading much sooner if I simply began reading and grading. I was, on the side and as a diversion—though really the task was consuming most of my thoughts because I was unwilling to commit to grading for the moment—making notes for a story-lecture I knew I wouldn't be delivering until the fall (and I anyway knew, because I would undoubtedly, in the intervening months, change my mind about the suitability of the subject of my notes or else forget why I'd wanted to talk about what I was taking notes on altogether by that point, I almost certainly would *not* tell the story I was then planning to tell, and would then have to devote all of my time—taking time away from my many other duties, in other words—to preparing, at the last minute and without considering it in the detail it deserved, the story-lecture I would *actually* give) when I heard the sound of what I would describe as an animal stuck in a small space and attempting to free itself above me. Given the situation, this was both deeply frustrating—how could I possibly grade these papers with so much noise going on? how could I possibly grade papers with an animal in the crawlspace or on the roof above me?—and something of a relief, since it gave me a better excuse not to begin reading and grading papers.

At first, I thought the noise must have been a squirrel on the roof—my office was on the top floor of the department's wing of the building, with a view of immense oak trees mostly hidden beyond the air conditioning condensers on the roof of the adjoining wing (in the other direction, behind a stand of low hedges and a fence overtaken by some sort of vine, I could also see the life sciences building, a much fancier and newer structure, whose offices were, I knew, outfitted with expensive ergonomic furniture, while we, in my department, still used mismatched office chairs that may as well have been purchased at a Goodwill, decades old, with gum stuck to their undersides, ripped vinyl upholstery, and weird, unidentifiable stains on their seats; the bottom drawer of my desk—a desk that had clearly been well used by other instructors before me—couldn't be opened, though I'd heard the rattling of something in it when the desk had first been moved into my office, and had often tried to pry it open, without success, to find out what was in it, what was making this noise), a cruel view, as it turned out, since my office seemed always to be five or six degrees warmer than those of my colleagues on lower floors of the building, which temperature students often complained loudly about as soon as they'd sat down across from me, as though I weren't also visibly sweating and uncomfortable. Being on the top floor meant that not only did I have this depressing view from my window but also that, when maintenance had to be done on the roof, I could hear not only the facilities workers walking around but even everything they said, and, besides, the rustling of the squirrels scrabbling overhead after leaping onto the roof from the huge magnolia south of the building's entrance. This sound, I thought, the one that had interrupted my not-reading and not-grading, didn't seem frantic enough to be a squirrel, or else its franticness wasn't sustained, as the squirrels' usually was. This noise was more sporadic—there would be a burst of the noise and then an uneasy, tense silence, and then, just when I thought maybe the thing, whatever it was, had freed itself and moved on, when I found myself, for instance, looking down at the first paper in the pile (with a title page, though a title page wasn't called for, and in a clear plastic binding, though this, too, wasn't called for), the noise would come back.

By this time, I'd abandoned my older, more practical lectures along with the quasi-lectures I'd delivered the semester I was working on my agglutinative English, in favor of what I called *stories*—it was, I thought, important to label them as such, to alert my listeners to their essentially false nature. After my brief experiments with speech-acts-language and agglutinative English, these *stories* seemed like much safer ground; they were, after all, really nothing more than parables, a means of communicating feelings and ideas that had existed for millennia. There was something appealing and even soothing about such a linguistic act; since all language was deceptive anyway, I'd thought, it seemed best, if one couldn't change the nature of language to instead advertise its deceitfulness up front, and, through doing that, at least partly reduce or attenuate its power to deceive. In fact, I thought of these stories as a kind of double negative; by employing intentionally and admittedly deceptive narrative, I could, I thought, get closer to the truth— by focusing outward instead of inward, by telling the stories of others instead of attempting to confess one's own story, I could, I thought, very possibly reach the heart of the matter and actually communicate something worthwhile. The telling of these stories would, then, not be subject to the same kinds of distortion that the speaking aloud of one's ideas, beliefs, or even one's history was, in the way that one's idea of the shape or size of a loved one's face is much closer to the objective truth of the thing than would be the loved one's idea of the shape or size of their own face, even when it's still not perfectly accurate. In order for this to work, though, the stories needed to be stories I had not myself come up with;

they had to be stories that already existed in the world. Telling such stories, communicating in this way, I thought, would then be a matter of selecting the correct story to express the particular idea, belief, or emotion I was attempting to communicate. If I tried to tell my wife why I'd decided we ought to keep some of our son's toys, my argument would, I knew, rely on things to which she had no access—my beliefs, opinions, tastes, emotions—and that therefore would have no power to affect her. But if I simply told her a story, I thought, one with which she might be somewhat familiar, I could perhaps get her to have some of the same emotions or beliefs I had, and by feeling those emotions or believing those beliefs, I could more thoroughly move her closer to my position and better show her how I was feeling and what I thought. It was a more perfect—more perfect because it took into account human nature as I knew it was, not as I thought it could or should be— version of my earlier attempt at speech-acts-language (that this speech-acts-language had always, in every situation, come across as either ridiculous (my wife) or obviously artificial (my colleagues), or even simply unintelligible (my students, as became clear almost immediately, and which result caused the speech-acts-language's speedy demise), and so I abandoned it relatively soon after I began it, though, with the agglutinative English, and because of my earlier failure with the speech-acts-language, I felt obligated to finish the semester still attempting it, at least in class). Although I'm not absolutely certain of this—ultimately, I didn't tell the story to my students, though this had less to do with me changing my mind about telling it than it did with the loss of my position at the university—I think, given the timing, the story-lecture I was working on instead of reading and grading papers that day was very likely the story of the burial shirt, or a variant of it meant to emphasize certain aspects of that story.

In that story, as my students would have heard, a mother loses her son when the boy is still a very young child, and when the father is away from home. I didn't remember any cause given for the death in the Grimms' version; the son, I think, just suddenly dies. The mother lies in bed, crying, long into the night, hour after hour, night after night, until eventually she loses her voice and becomes seriously ill, and when the father returns home, he finds that his son is missing and his wife can't speak and won't respond to his questions. She's weeping silently and without any tears falling, facing the wall. He tries everything, but she just stares at the wall through her invisible tears and won't even look at him, and, just as he's about to leave the house to go searching for his son, a neighbor appears at the door and explains that she has come because she's concerned that his wife might be in trouble. Since the burial, and until today, the neighbor says, the mother has been crying, wailing and sobbing without stopping—all of the neighbors have heard it—and so, when the house finally fell silent, that silence worried the neighbors. Could the mother have harmed herself or come to some grief? The husband says that, no, fortunately, she's still alive, she's in the corner, weeping, he thinks, though there are no tears, and she looks ill and won't speak to him, won't even acknowledge him. He shows the neighbor his wife, focused on the corner of the kitchen where their son used to play in the mornings when the sun barely rose above the horizon and the snow was deep outside, and asks, *What burial?* The neighbor says *No. This is not good.* She tells the husband what has happened, and what is now happening: *Your son died,* she tells the husband, *and now your wife's tears won't leave him at peace. He is soaked in these tears and has come to tell her to please dry her eyes so that he can rest.* The father, overcome with grief, demands the neighbor tell him where his son is buried, and he immediately sets off with a shovel to dig up the grave. In the tiny casket, he finds his son, in his white burial shirt, drenched even though it hasn't rained in days and the ground all around is dry, and so, intending to replace the shirt with a clean, dry one and the leaking casket with a new casket that won't leak, he brings his son back home where he puts the boy in his bed and immediately begins building this new casket. The mother, meanwhile, still hasn't moved, and doesn't realize her son—or her son's body—is in the house. I think at some point I realized the story might be too grisly to tell my students and would almost certainly result in a complaint being lodged against me, followed by a meeting with the chair—who would try to be sensitive, given the subject matter, but who would, in the end, turn more decisively against me; it had been over a year, she would say, and this is completely inappropriate, and how could you not see this is completely inappropriate, and we (meaning the department) have offered grief counseling but now we have to insist you go to therapy or we'll have to terminate your contract—and possibly even a second meeting with the chair, with the dean in attendance, but I'm sure at the time, in my office with the sound interrupting me, I at least tried to make it work, maybe by focusing on the period after the mother had fallen silent and the father had returned home but before the neighbor's arrival, but then the noise came back and I lost my train of thought altogether.

I remember I stood up and looked at the outside wall of the building, from which direction I then realized the sound was coming; not, I mean, from above me at all, but from the top of the outside wall where it met the roof. I looked up at the arched clerestory window there and saw what I thought must be a hummingbird ramming itself into the window; I would realize later that, without meaning to, I was holding my breath. Because the noise had been recurring at odd intervals for maybe as long as ten or even fifteen minutes, I think I must have wondered that this bird could still manage to launch itself at the window. Wasn't there some sort of threshold for self-inflicted pain in all living organisms, including birds? Though the window hadn't been cleaned since I'd occupied the office, I thought I could see a stain there I hadn't seen before, and I thought that if the hummingbird or whatever it was had left a stain of itself on the window, at some level, surely, it must have realized what it was doing wasn't good for it. For some reason, I remember I thought about the dinosaurs just then, about, specifically, the Alvarez impact, about the abrupt change in the world the Alvarezes had seen. It seems possible, I think, that this line of thinking led me, eventually, to that feeling of doom I had

had when confronted with the bowl in the Macy's—it's a strange connection to make, I know, but I think it's one I *did* make—and, obviously, this had to do with me telling my son about the Alvarez impact, since, though he had had a passing interest in dinosaurs, it was really just a passing interest—he would have been, I think, still much too young for anything more; his interest in the neighbor's dogs had been much, much greater, for instance—and, even if he had been truly obsessed by the subject, he still might not have been interested in Alvarez and his hypothesis, much less in the reaction of the so-called *scientific community* to that hypothesis, which, as I've already said, was what I focused on when I told him about the hypothesis and the dinosaurs (which dinosaurs, come to think of it, I almost failed to mention, almost as though I were going out of my way *not* to mention them, like I was ashamed of them, or ashamed of their deaths).

This bird ramming itself into the window made me nervous in some way: It wasn't, I thought, that I empathized with or thought of myself as somehow related to the bird—I couldn't really see the bird when it hit the window, and anyway the window was far from clean—but maybe instead it was that I thought, in those moments, there was something inescapably emblematic (emblematic, I mean, of something in my own life, I guess) in the bird's behavior, something that meant, maybe especially for me, that something *else*, something worse, was on the way for us, like the splat of the first few fat raindrops on the sidewalk signaling the possibility of a storm, and I found myself trying to think through this idea—along with the outline of the story-lecture I'd just been planning, and of course how to deal with my wife when, inevitably, I returned home to find her sitting at the kitchen table, silent and unresponsive—but also distracted as though the bird was colliding with me rather than with the window.

Because I'm stubborn, I stayed at my desk for another ten minutes while the hummingbird rammed itself into the window and I did no work; it was, I think, less a matter of doing something to help the bird than of deciding not to try to ignore it that I resisted, but then I had to go to the bathroom, or so I told myself. The bathroom nearest my office, which had been closed earlier that morning but which I thought, since I assumed it had been closed for cleaning, would, by this point, be open again, was still closed, and I noticed a smell coming from it, and so I went down to the next floor, where the building opened out under my window and where the chair of the department, a woman who, when I'd first been hired, had been friendly and solicitous, but who, after the first student complaint, had turned cold and who always now seemed to have something better to do than to speak to me, had her office. The fire door to the rooftop below my window had been propped open, I saw, with an orange rubber warning cone with *Facilities and Maintenance* written on it in Sharpie, and I heard the sound of someone moving around outside, a man, as it turned out, with a long pole with a net on the end, like a pool skimmer. I'd never seen this man before—I didn't think he was someone with an office in the building—but it was clear that he wasn't part of the facilities department; they all wore uniforms, and this man was in a button-down shirt with a patterned tie. Because, I guess, nothing better occurred to me to say, I asked if everything was all right, which, of course, was a dumb thing to ask—the man was obviously exerting himself far beyond his capabilities (he was short and stocky, with stubby arms), and the fact that I'd never seen him in the building before meant he probably didn't usually do whatever it was he was doing, at least, not here—but, still, in the moment, it was all that came to me to say. He continued watching the bird, however, and although I could read the cues he was giving me to get lost, because I dreaded returning to my office and to my worries about my wife more than I dreaded making a bad impression on this man—who, in any case, with his sweat-soaked armpits and his shirt coming untucked and riding up his belly, I felt, couldn't really look so far down upon me if he even looked down on me at all—I stayed standing in the doorway until he said, *Yes, yes,* he was all right, and then I opened the door all the way, being careful to leave the worn orange cone in its place, and stepped out onto the roof, looking up to where the skimmer's net wavered in the air.

I had nothing else to say, so I asked, absurdly, whether the man was trying to catch the bird. This question, I thought, surprised him more than it should have—it was obvious that he was trying to catch the bird, so I could understand disbelief (what a stupid question!), but he reacted like I'd asked him what the cafeteria was serving for lunch today, or where I could get a good haircut. *Bird?* he asked. I noticed the pattern of his tie was the university's logo miniaturized and arranged in elaborate whorls that looked vaguely wintry or holiday-themed, and I thought briefly about asking the man whether the department had offered to replace his tie with a rebranded tie (we were, just then, in the middle of a so-called *university-wide rebranding*, which really only meant that all of the boxes of stationery in the copy room were now said to be off-limits, since they had the old letterhead, but of course, even a semester into this *rebranding*, no new stationery had arrived to replace the old stationery, which meant that everyone in the department simply continued to use the old stationery and occasionally the chair would send out an email asking us all to please stop using the old stationery, which was nonetheless left in the copy room where it had always been left; only the chair had access to stationery with the new logo and she never offered any of it to us), but I thought better of this joke when I got a close look at his face—damp with sweat, bruised circles under his eyes, slack lips—and then I noticed the strange noise the bird above us was making, a whirring getting louder, and the fact that it kept landing and pausing before launching itself again into the air, and that's when I realized it wasn't a bird at all.

In my memory—even at the time, I think—the thing, the not-bird, was really only a blur, even when it dropped down almost to our level, on the top of one of the condensers. It was too blocky and large to be any bird I'd ever seen, I thought, and so, despite its movement and the noise it had been making, it very clearly wasn't a hummingbird. The man with the skimmer slowly pulled the pole through his hands until he was almost gripping it at the net, and then he dropped the net over the thing and scooped it over the side of the condenser and twisted the net over itself so that the thing inside couldn't get out. *Excuse me*, the man said, hustling the net and the thing around me and back through the fire door. He kicked the orange cone out of the way as he went through the door, and so I had to jerk forward at the last moment to grab the edge of the door to keep it from closing and locking me out of the building, on the roof.

I wanted to follow him and I wanted to forget the encounter altogether—not because it was demeaning to be treated in that way, though it was, of course, but because, even then, I think, I recognized that the thing I'd seen, the thing I'd thought was a bird but now thought wasn't a bird, was something of great importance, a thing I really didn't want to see again. I tried to return to my notes on the burial shirt story-lecture, but I found I couldn't focus, and my thoughts drifted to this thing, this not-bird, which, because my thoughts at the time were almost always consumed by thoughts of my son, began to sort of fuse with thoughts of my son, and I think I started to imagine that the two were somehow connected, in the way, I mean, that, late at night, after you've seen a scary movie about a killer in someone's house, you might connect a creak in the floorboards of your own house to an intruder, especially if you'd had such an intruder before, even though the creak's true cause might be the dog stepping on the floorboards in the other room, or the house, old as it is, settling, or else might not even *be* the floorboards at all but some other noise altogether. I only mean that, because the not-bird and thoughts of my son had occurred at more or less the same time, my mind couldn't avoid trying to find some correspondence between the two things, even as my mind struggled to convince itself that there was no such correspondence.

In Which
He Attempts to Describe His Work

Although I'm sure it must seem strange to speak about my work in this context—that I might have ulterior motives in doing so, I guess, must seem obvious (though I don't myself believe that's why these two things occur to me at once and together)—I had, at the time of the accident, almost completely put aside the project I'd been working on, my survey of the language spoken by the so-called Man of the Hole, the last surviving member of an Amazonian tribe that had had no outside contact in living memory until its discovery by the Brazilian government. (And as frustrating as this work had been—being the last member of his tribe, observers said, he'd barely spoken at all (who would he have spoken to beyond threatening the officials who'd wandered onto his land?), and the government had taken the official stance that he shouldn't be disturbed (this was after he'd threatened officials with an axe they'd left on one of their earlier visits), so no further work could be done without a change in the government's position, and, besides, the university would only pledge funds that were wholly inadequate to even the relatively modest study I'd proposed, and would only pledge those funds after I'd shamed them into it by presenting my work to the Brazilian Student's Union, a surprisingly large and powerful group on campus—still, the work I took up after the accident was, if anything, *more* frustrating, so much so that I found myself constantly tempted to give up my new, impossible project and return to the survey, to the hours of watching the same few videos over and over, if only so that, even when the scholarship I produced was speculative to an irresponsible degree (for example, my theorized relationship between it and a poorly documented and obscure language spoken only by the shaman of a very small indigenous tribe of the Paraguayan Gran Chaco, a theory based on a single utterance in the video a FUNAI crew had shot during one of their earliest visits I took to mean *danger* or *caution*, but which utterance would, in the language of these shaman, also have meant something like *the state of being on one's own*, and, oddly, *the distress caused by eating spoiled food*, and which utterance ultimately, might only, I knew, have been the man's attempt to communicate with an outsider, using what he thought of as *their* language), I could at least publish *something*, and, through publishing *something*, maybe somehow get a better job, a job where I could teach my area of expertise instead of freshman survey courses, or even just a job where I didn't have to wait on the results of student evaluations to know whether I'd be employed the following year.) Although my job was the teaching of the study of language and of its use, or maybe *because* my job was the teaching of the study of language and of its use, I had, long ago, lost faith in what most language did—what, I guess, I'd realized most language was *capable* of doing, which is to say, nothing much, or else something both very fleeting and very weak (and so maybe also, I'd once thought, something therefore beautiful, in the way that beauty is itself often fleeting and superfluous; the moment I kept coming back to in the videos was the moment in which the Man of the Hole seemed to be singing, though he had to know no one hearing him would understand anything he was singing, and anyway how did one find the strength to sing after all of his family, every single one of his friends, enemies, neighbors—*everyone he'd ever known*—had been slaughtered? How was such a thing possible?). It wasn't that I hadn't always known that talk didn't add up to much, but that, before, I'd fooled myself into thinking there was at least one setting—academia—where it still had currency and value, and then, after I'd worked in academia for a while and gradually stopped producing the kind of scholarship others in my field produced (occasionally, still, an acquaintance would ask me to send or present something about my

theory out of, I got the impression, a sense of professional duty to
our shared mentors, and always I had to say I had nothing ready to
publish or present, and otherwise I was left on my own), I realized
that academia was like every other setting, really just another office
job, a disappointingly political and ultimately worthless profession
whose most successful exemplars were really interested only in getting and wielding power, and this naturally caused both an extended bout of depression and my abandonment of the survey, a survey
I'd been working on, as much as was possible, for years, as part of
the dissertation I was supposed to be finishing (eventually I abandoned also the methods I'd devised for that research, methods, I'd
thought, that could be of real help to forensic linguists and scholars
of vanishing languages of which only fragments were extant, and
which methods, I'd once believed, would be my real contribution
to the discipline), and that abandonment therefore affected me in
several consequential ways, by which I mean, in part, that I not
only stopped writing in my rare moments of so-called *research time*
(evenings, weekends, holidays, breaks), but that I also lost all faith
in my curricula, in the lectures I'd planned to give, the assignments
I'd set my students, my methods of evaluating those assignments,
the purpose of education, everything. Still, though, I spoke.

But then there was the accident, and, afterward, I remember
my wife getting angry with me because I wasn't talking, not even
when she or the social worker asked me direct questions, not even
when circumstances—my mostly silent eulogy comes to mind—
demanded I speak. I can remember that I thought—I can remember this because I still think it, and so it's less a matter of remembering than of recognizing that this way of thinking must have
had a beginning—that language was, at its core, deceitful in the
extreme, because it relied on an understanding of the movement
of time that incited its speakers to a specious kind of inductive
reasoning; just the act of retroactively recounting some event or
action—which is, after all, the most typical use of language—was
always really an attempt on the part of the person doing that recounting to give meaning to an otherwise meaningless act they'd

already carried out (because the other option was, I guess, to despair that there was no meaning to anything one did, or, as I had, to accept that nothing meant anything anyway and that language simply added this layer of deception to the other layers of which existence was, ultimately, made), and that this was really the *only* purpose of language, as far as I could tell, to give an illusion of meaning where, manifestly, no such meaning existed. Still, I had no alternative in mind, and I went completely without speaking for probably four or five days straight, nearly a week (there was then the eulogy and the odd feeling of sound coming from my throat and my mouth). In any case, I think this—*this* meaning my period of muteness—marked a decisive change in my behavior, if not in my thinking, and it was during this period of muteness that I conceived of my speech-acts-language, a language whose elements weren't intended to *mean* anything but instead, on their own, to accomplish things, to promise future action or consummate present intention, and then the speech-acts-language, after its nearly immediate demise, led to my failed attempt at an agglutinative English, and the agglutinative English, eventually, to the story-lectures.

Because the accident happened during the semester, and because my wife and I couldn't afford an extended leave, when I returned to class, I delivered almost two full weeks of classes in my speech-acts-language. Despite signs that my students weren't responding to it at all well (which would, I knew, mean that some of them would have already gone to the chair or their advisors to complain), still, I thought, eventually, they would see the value of this language in which there was no dissembling, shifting of blame, or invention of causality, and so I kept at it. When, at the end of the second week of this—by then, we would have been approaching finals—one of my students took a bottle of Xanax and died in his dorm room (he was one of ten students to commit suicide on campus that month, I think), I saw that his suicide would give the chair the pretext she needed to *review my teaching practices* (meaning that the chair herself or a colleague sympathetic to the chair's

position would come to the next session for *an observation*), and
so I knew I would have to find some way of incorporating more
traditional classroom practices into these speech-acts-language lectures or else I would, sooner rather than later, be forced to explain
the way they worked to the chair, who would, naturally, refuse to
even attempt to understand the way they worked no matter how
they were explained to her and almost certainly insist I take the
extended leave my wife and I couldn't afford.

But then it's important to note that even before the accident
and my ensuing silence, I'd already had the loss of faith in language
I've mentioned and had been searching for some way to speak to
others that didn't seem completely dishonest to me, and this search
had led to speech patterns that, I realize now, could only have been
off-putting to others, in particular my wife, my students, and the
chair, who'd called me in for a meeting the day of the accident
ostensibly to talk about a complaint a student had lodged about
an unfair grade, but which meeting, because of the way I had, by
then, determined to speak, I knew wouldn't go well, because the
chair, I knew, would insist on an explanation, and I could only
refuse to give one.

I couldn't have slept well the night before; though I remember
by then I already placed so little importance on the words I and
others spoke, I knew the chair felt very differently, and so I could
only have felt some anxiety about how I would conduct myself in
this meeting. It might also have been a night my wife woke me
to tell me she'd heard noises, or one in which she'd talked in her
sleep, I can't now remember exactly, but I do remember that it was
hot and humid that morning and the windows of the car (and my
glasses) fogged up almost instantly after I'd turned the key in the
ignition, and I would have been in a hurry because the argument
I'd refused to have with my wife—often, as was the case that morning, it was quicker to *have* the argument than to try to maintain
our fragile peace, since these arguments were really pretexts for
my wife or myself to say something to each other that otherwise
couldn't have been said, and which thing, once said, we would later

attempt to excuse by saying it had been something we didn't really mean to say and that had only been said in the heat of the moment (even when, much later, those same things would frequently be borne out as our true feelings, the ones we'd dreaded admitting to having), but, even so, I usually tried to avoid these arguments, if only so that later I could deny there had been any real disagreement, in order to put off further argument; that morning, I think I recall, we were (I was) not-arguing about our son's pre-K, or, since he wouldn't be old enough for pre-K for a few years, not-arguing about the possibilities for our son's pre-K, and I think my own position was something like, because it wasn't a thing we would really have to worry about for a few years, it seemed better, at that moment, to not worry about it, and to see where we were when the time came, with the hope that we would be in a better position (it would be hard to be in a worse position, I remember thinking, which thought shows just how poor my foresight was), and I was struggling to explain all of this in a way I thought would be comprehensible but would also not violate my convictions about language and its inherent deceitfulness, and my wife wasn't simply frustrated but actually crying in anger that I wouldn't, as she said, *Talk like normal, act like normal*, and she was already threatening to take our son, who had meanwhile climbed over the gate on the patio, maybe to her father's, and not come back until I had *gotten help*—had dragged on until finally I'd had to get up from the table to remind my wife I had this meeting in thirty minutes, and so, unless there was absolutely no traffic and I somehow got the best parking space, either of which, individually, was extremely unlikely, and both of which, together, were next-to-impossible to imagine happening, I would be late for the meeting, and the chair would take the opportunity to refer my case to the Learning Center, meaning that I would then have to stay late on days that I taught to attend lectures on how to *communicate more effectively* given by inarticulate people who'd never taught and who tended to type everything they were going to say on slides and then read everything on those slides aloud even as those slides were being displayed behind them on the screen, and this was, as I thought I wouldn't need to say, a thing I wanted very much to avoid.

The fact that the windows in the car and my glasses fogged up immediately meant, I knew, that I would have to wait until the air inside the car had dried out enough that the windows cleared and I could see through the windows, and this in turn meant sitting there in the car with the A/C going full blast, but my wife was at the car door, still furious with me, telling me to roll down the goddamned window, and I was thinking that, if I did so, it would take that much longer for the windows to finally clear so that I could leave, but that if I didn't, I would only make her angrier and would spend the entire day feeling guilty for the way I'd treated her, so I rolled down the window and she told me to go on, go to work, but before I came home, I should call her and tell her what I was going to do differently, how I was going to change myself, or else I shouldn't come home at all, and I could see, from her expression, that much of her anger was actually fear, and, making what I thought of as an apologetic face and pointing at my wrist as though there was a watch there, I tried to take her hand with my pointing hand, and she pulled back violently and turned away, and so, after a pause, I looked at the outer rims of the side-view mirrors (the only parts of those mirrors that weren't, themselves, also fogged up; I remember a vaguely bird-shaped spot on the driver's side mirror that hadn't fogged up, small and bird-shaped or duck-shaped, though, maybe, I'd thought, if looked at from the right angle, maybe instead tear-shaped or whale-shaped), and backed out of the driveway as slowly as I could, looking both ways down the street but still unable to see directly behind me or anywhere around the car, and that's when I felt one of the back tires roll over something, my son.

He Meets the Entomologist Again

It hadn't been so difficult to locate the man with the net I'd seen on the roof in the faculty directory on the university's website—as a condition of employment, I'd had to sit for a headshot in front of an elementary-school-picture-day background, had even been forced to smile (the photographer wouldn't take the picture until I'd smiled, I remember, and couldn't seem to get my name right, even though it's a relatively common name), and of course I knew I wasn't the only one who'd been made to demean myself solely so that some administrator somewhere could say they did something worth doing, so I knew this man's photo would appear on the university's website—though, despite knowing his obvious interests (the bird-thing), I'd looked in anthropology before I realized I really ought to be looking in biology, and then there he was, in among the biology department's *Faculty and Staff*, standing in front of a familiar textured-blue-gradient background, with his campus phone number, email, and office listed next to that photo above his few publications, all indicating that his specialty was entomology—*Hempitera*, I remember reading, *Cicadoidea*, I remember reading.

As far as I can recall, sometime after the incident with the bird-thing on the roof (this was, in fact, I think, one of the papers I was trying to make myself grade that day), I saw that one of my Intro students had plagiarized a third or more of his paper; for one thing, nothing in his paper resembled the assignment he'd been given and for another, the passage he'd plagiarized had clearly been rogeted—which is to say that he'd run the text he'd stolen through a piece of software that automatically plugged in more or less randomly cho-sen synonyms for each of the words in the original passage, result-ing in a word salad I struggled not to applaud (*It is solely in a style that I am able to degrade something by something*, he'd written; I'd wondered whether he was winking at me) but that was also mostly unreadable—and, as a result of this discovery, I'd been forced to bring the paper and the student who'd turned it in before the panel charged with investigating such infractions of the student code of ethics. The panel met—this was weeks later, nearer the end of the semester, when, I guess, the university could be certain of the re-ceipt of this student's tuition—in a small, coffin-shaped room with whiteboards on every wall. The administrative assistant I checked in with was probably a student, I thought, in part because of his age and in part because he listened to me say my name and then did absolutely nothing with it, didn't write it down or speak it into the telephone or get up to relay the information to anyone else, just continued sitting at the desk. I sat down across from the desk in one of the yellow vinyl-covered chairs there, and, with nothing else to do, looked at the papers I'd printed out, the student's paper and the website I'd found by substituting what I guessed, based on the rogeted text, had been in the original passages. A man, some functionary with a title like Assistant Vice Dean of Student Affairs, came out and told me he would be acting as a liaison between the panel and the charging party (by which he of course meant me, though he didn't indicate this in any way). He told me there was another waiting room on the other side of the room the panel was meeting in, outside of Student Counseling, and that I was free to use this room (though, because the panel was in session, I would have to exit the building, walk around the corner, and enter the building on the other side in order to get to it), and this, I remem-ber, made me feel as though I'd somehow sat down in the wrong waiting room—why would he mention the other room if I was already waiting in the right place?—even though the administra-tive assistant I was supposed to check in with was located in this waiting room, and his office (the office of this man who was acting as a liaison) was just off *this* waiting room. As I'd seen through the window when I'd passed it, there was no administrative assistant in the waiting room outside of Student Counseling, and so really no reason at all to use this other waiting room, and so I hadn't used it, but now, I remember, this man's insistence that I *could* use it made me doubt whether I'd chosen the right waiting room after all. Was there something about this other waiting room that would have somehow benefited me more than the waiting room in which I was already waiting did? It wasn't long before a member of the panel came to get me—I didn't know how he could know which of the two waiting rooms I was waiting in, because the student administrative assistant still seemed to be watching some video on the computer on the desk in front of him, a street magician in regular clothes but with conspicuously gelled hair performing tricks with a candy bar, from what I could see over the desk—and so much effort had been put into informing me that there was this other waiting room I *could* use that I thought maybe it was a signal that I'd be looked for in that waiting room first and then only after it had been determined I wasn't there would anyone look for me here and the whole system seemed indicative of the way the university was run: instructors had tiny, un-air-conditioned offices with old furniture, classes met in storage closets and conference rooms, but administrators had multiple, redundant waiting rooms.

The student who'd plagiarized his paper, I ought to say, wasn't present because he had, I was told, *chosen not to attend*, though really this seemed like a strange way of putting things; it wasn't as though he was lodging a protest against the fairness or legitimacy of the process; this (*chosen not to attend*) was, I thought, really just a way of phrasing things that spared the *charged party*—this was how the student was referred to during the hearing—some bit of embarrassment, I thought, at being shown to want to avoid responsibility for his past actions. In any case, although the student wasn't there, this man, the one I'd discovered was an entomologist—a man with a faint South African accent I hadn't noticed on the roof, maybe because he'd said so little—*was* there, seated on this panel, was, in fact, the chair of the panel, and so he was the person in the room who ought to have asked the most questions or at least the most important questions, but, in reality, he'd only asked me, before the boilerplate language of the panel's commission could be read into the record by the graduate student representative, if there was an opening statement I'd like to make, and then, after I'd said *No*, he rushed through the rest of the process as though there were many other things he'd rather be doing, an attitude that was, to me, completely understandable and not at all unreasonable, given the timing of this hearing, but which seemed to bother not only the earnest graduate student who frowned every time I said anything, but also the other faculty members on the panel, who all exchanged looks, and one of them, a woman who didn't introduce herself but who I knew was a faculty member and not a student because I'd seen her at the winter graduation, on the stage with the rest of her department (Education, maybe?) and I remembered I'd thought she looked a lot like my date to my high school senior prom, just with ears that stuck out from the sides of her face, maybe because of the cap she was wearing or how she was wearing it, cleared her throat very loudly several times, to the point that the man sitting next to her asked if she needed water.

After I'd declined to give an opening statement, I was asked to summarize my case, but instead I fell silent, first wondering of what, beyond a summary of the case—here's the student's paper, here's my syllabus with its university-mandated language about plagiarism, here's the source from which the material has been copied, here are the factors that played into my suspicion that the material hadn't originated with the student (all of which materials I'd submitted, in writing, weeks earlier, and which written submission I foolishly thought should have made this in-person meeting unnecessary)—my opening statement, had I chosen to give one, would have consisted, and then, when I could see my silence was making everyone in the room uncomfortable, I cleared my throat slowly, and thought about telling them the only story that then came to mind, a story that had been on my mind often at that time, the story of Pinocchio. I couldn't decide where to start my story—Collodi's novel starts with the wood Geppetto uses to make Pinocchio jumping out of its basket and hitting the man who sold it to Geppetto in the shin, I remembered, but I knew I couldn't start the story there; no one would understand why I was telling such a story if I started there, and yet, to start with Pinocchio's hanging, or with Pinocchio smashing the talking cricket against the wall, or even with Pinocchio grabbing Geppetto's wig wouldn't have served my purpose any better, and so I stayed silent and tried to decide what exactly I wanted to tell them; what I most wanted to tell them was, in fact, that Collodi had been so disappointed in the ending he wrote that later he claimed not to remember writing it at all, sometimes pretending he hadn't written it, that it had been written by someone else—and because I wasn't talking and the entomologist wasn't talking, it seemed no one else felt free to speak, either, and so everyone just shuffled the papers in front of them, copies of the student's paper and my report, as though seriously considering their contents for the first time, and, when I cleared my throat a second time, I noticed an armadillo digging around in the dirt just outside the window, maybe three feet from the entomologist's right elbow, and I remember wondering if this was a sign of rabies, that the armadillo was out during the day, and I also remember thinking the building must be the last building on this end of the campus before the immense wild area that was part of the university's land holdings but which the university didn't really want or need, and then, just when I'd decided to tell them about Lampwick, watching for the Coachman and telling Pinocchio about the Land of Toys where there was no homework, no school at all, the entomologist suddenly broke the long, tense silence and said *A few years back*. I couldn't have been the only one to jump (though using that expression obviously overstates things; I didn't *jump* really, I just flinched, violently, in my chair, which was one of those rolling office chairs with almost no back support and which creaked loudly when I flinched) when he said this, though of course he kept talking through my spasm, *an ice cream place in Missouri made ice cream with cicadas—what people here call locusts, though they aren't locusts, locusts are something else altogether* (his pronunciation of *altogether*, in particular, sounded South African to me)—*dipped in brown sugar and chocolate.* (And all of this was, needless to say, a complete non sequitur, having nothing at all to do with the student's plagiarized paper.) *They sold out of this ice cream,* he said, *but they didn't make another batch because the health department advised them against it and probably because it was near the end of the life cycle, and so there wouldn't have been many more cicadas to serve. Obviously, they would have been warned not to try to serve any of the cicadas collected after they were already dead—contamination, you know?—but, from what I understand—and think of how nice and crunchy!—even though by then you'd think there would have been a bunch of them on trees and buildings, I guess they didn't consider serving the moultings. That's a little strange, eh?*

I had a thought—really, in the situation, the only thought, I think, that made any sense—that was not or did not seem to be the end product of any deductive or inductive process, but which was instead a very sudden thing, like a revelation or maybe a memory of something I'd completely forgotten coming suddenly to mind, that the man's long silence and the very strange remark with which he ended that silence must have both had something to do with the bird-thing he'd trapped on the roof that day, which, in turn, is to say that, in that moment, and not only simply because I'd met this man in two situations only, once on the roof and now here, again, I assumed that the bird-thing (which I then realized must have been an insect, or at least something this man suspected to be an insect, not, I mean, a bird at all, which might have interested a zoologist or an ornithologist, but not this man, an entomologist—and later, of course, all of this was confirmed) was the cause of his distracted and disordered thoughts, even though, clearly, I couldn't know this with any certainty. He was preoccupied, though, not oblivious—he could see that his very strange remark had mystified the panel and its guest, me, and so, seeming somewhat embarrassed, he asked a question about the plagiarized paper, though his question, I remember, now, strangely, seemed just as out of place and inappropriate as the ice cream remark had, in part *because* of the ice cream remark and because he seemed not to notice what he'd just said, and, because I was still thinking about the ice cream remark—what I was thinking, as I remember it, or anyway what I was trying to think about, was whether the ice cream thing might somehow have been a clue that this man was giving me, a hint as to which way I ought to answer his question, or, really, the panel's questions, though no one else had yet spoken—and because I was still unnerved by the silence that had preceded it and was still worried, somewhere in the back of my mind, that something I'd done had caused either the silence or the strange remark or both, that, when he'd asked his question, I struggled, really struggled, to find an answer that wouldn't embarrass either him or me. *From the charged party's name and from his way of writing, I'd guess he's Brazilian. Do you think that might explain this?* he'd asked.

I looked around the room at the confused, pinched faces of the students and faculty members on the panel; I couldn't have been the only person there to have been worried that any answer I gave to such a question, short of condemning the question as bigoted, would be construed as in some way endorsing the prejudice that seemed to inform it. I don't much like confrontation, and so my response—which would have been more effective coming immediately after the question, rather than, as it in fact did, almost a full minute after, when it really seemed as though I'd tried and failed to come up with a better (better in the sense of better defusing the situation, or better in the sense of better deflecting and even abdicating my obligation to answer) response—my response, *I'm not sure I understand the question*, was, typically for me, inadequate and really only demonstrated my moral cowardice, though I think most of the panel members were still too shocked and disgusted by what this man had said to notice that I wasn't challenging him on the presumptions inherent in his question. Not, of course, that it was or should have been solely my duty to challenge him—in the setting, and given my lack of familiarity with him and the panel, I think really I was probably the last person (of those present) who ought to have challenged him, though I can also acknowledge that this thought might be self-justification—just that I, because he'd addressed his question to me, had been given the best opportunity to challenge him, and had, as I had so often in the past, failed to take that opportunity.

Still, though, no one else in the room spoke. The entomologist finally pushed back from the table, stood up, and, leaving his binder of papers in front of his chair, walked first to the whiteboard jammed in the corner of the tiny room, then left the room altogether, leaving the rest of us looking down at our own binders and then up at each other, more or less in shock. Eventually, the graduate student—a little person with a very tight V-neck sweater in the school colors—who'd been in charge of reading the boilerplate to begin the hearing read the boilerplate to end the hearing, and I was told that I could go, which I then did. Though I can't remember what I did after the hearing but before I finally left campus—I really don't think I did much work, though I feel certain I went back to my office—I do remember that that day was also the day all of the traffic lights on the highway home were out, or else what I remember is that the fact that all of them were out, on the same afternoon, seemed very strange, not to say ominous, because it also meant that most of the city had lost power, and of course how long it had taken to get home, because other drivers still seemed not to understand what to do when a light had gone out, even though, across the city, power outages, as I've already mentioned, had, by then, become much more common—not only, at that time of the year, was there torrential rain most days and so also, often, flash flooding, but there were besides, any time a heavy thunderstorm passed through, tornado warnings, tornado watches, and occasionally an actual tornado—and so some drivers simply stopped where the dead lights hung overhead and allowed everyone else in the intersection to go, and wouldn't move until there was a critical mass of drivers honking at them to go, so that, when they finally went, they did so apparently under considerable stress, and sometimes as a result neglected to check whether other drivers at the intersection were already themselves entering the intersection, and so, inevitably, there were also accidents, and there were no traffic cops anymore or anyway no cops who responded to accidents, and so there would then be confusion about who could go around while the drivers of the cars involved took photos of each other's cars as they'd been when they'd collided, still in the intersection, and then a fistfight or screaming match when the shock of the thing had worn off and the adrenaline had kicked in, and all the other drivers who slowed or stopped to look and to yell.

When I pulled up in the driveway, the house was dark, as had been most of the houses in our neighborhood (though not our next-door neighbors, both of whom I could hear, had their generators going), and my wife was sitting at the kitchen table in the dark, looking at her phone, and the house was besides much warmer than usual—it was very hot out and the air conditioner ran all day long most days—which I guessed meant that the power had been out there for some time. My wife, I knew, would only have gotten home maybe a half hour before me, so, even though I asked how long the power had been out, I didn't really expect an answer. She didn't know how long it had been out at the house but she told me the power had gone out at her office three or four times that day, and she'd left early, and this answer meant, I realized immediately, that my own story—*All the lights out! The whole way home!*—wasn't really significant; what she was telling me, or what she could have told me, had she seemed less unfriendly in that moment (a word—*unfriendly*—that, now that I've used it, seems unfair to her; I think I only really mean that she didn't seem herself, though of course I understand why she didn't), was more interesting, more consequential than what I could tell her. For some reason, I hadn't thought about telling her about the hearing or the strange behavior of the entomologist, only about the power outage, the lights, the accidents, and now that I'd found out this wouldn't be news to her, I couldn't think of anything to say whatsoever. She was still staring at her cell phone. She asked whether I was getting any service. By this point, it occurred to me later, really almost all of the time we spent together was either in bed, asleep, or at the dining room table, the television on to drown out any conversation, both of us looking at our phones. It was a situation I had, before the accident, often wanted to change, but which, since the accident, I'd stopped even registering. *I hope this doesn't last too long*, I remember saying (it was, I thought, clear that I meant the power outage). I tried to find a comfortable place to sit where I wouldn't feel watched, or maybe a place where I wouldn't feel conspicuously *not* watched, while my wife kept looking at her phone, waiting for service, I guess.

A Stranger Is Once Again Mentioned

Not that night but *another* night when the power was out, a few weeks later, was the night the man who must have been the man who'd broken in before broke in again. I mean that it seems unlikely that two different men—or more than two, I guess; this had been going on for some time, according to my wife, even though she'd only recently learned that it wasn't me—would have been breaking into our house but not taking anything, and at about the same time of night. This time, my wife woke up and then rolled over and woke me up, and, even with the neighbor's generator going a few feet away from the bedroom window, I could hear someone moving around, a little clumsy, in the living room. After the last break-in, my wife bought herself a Taser—the one on sale was pink and looked like a small flashlight, and even though the clerk assured us it was exactly the same, my wife insisted on paying nearly twice the price of the pink one to get the one in black, which, again, was otherwise identical—but I didn't know where she kept the thing, and she didn't offer it to me when I got up. I remember I'd thought about buying a baseball bat when we were at the sporting goods store buying the Taser, but I felt silly doing it—I was thinking about bringing it to the register with the Taser, about having it rung up—and decided to maybe do that later, when my wife wasn't around to see me buying a baseball, too, or a glove, for cover, and then, a few nights before this break-in—the one I'm describing now—I remember I'd thought I heard a noise just as I was falling asleep, and I told myself I'd find something in the

house (a wrench, a curtain rod, something) that I could put next
to the bed, but then I decided to do that later, too, and then I just
went to sleep, so, that night, the night of the outage, there wasn't
anything for me to take with me to the living room when I went
to see what was making the noise and I saw, in the dim glow of our
neighbor's porch lights (the street lights were out because of the
power outage, but the moon was bright and our neighbor's porch
lights shone directly into our living room window), the silhouette
of a man standing in front of our refrigerator. I was, of course, terrified, but I can remember thinking that, with the power out, the
longer this person held the door open, the more food would spoil,
and though I couldn't form the words to say anything, I think I
must have kind of lunged forward a few steps, probably to close
the refrigerator door, before stopping myself and instead making
a dry clicking sound with my throat—I was, I remember, trying
to ask what this person was doing but I couldn't speak at first—
and then, when it was clear from the shape of the silhouette that
the person was facing me, holding something out in front of him,
I could finally say *What are you doing?* (I'd meant to add *here*, I
think, *What are you doing here?* even though that's also an awkward
way to phrase my question, implying that I'd expected this person
somewhere else, just not *here* (which wasn't the case)) to which
this person answered *There's no time for that* in a way that made it
seem as though he was mocking me and imitating my voice, just
at a slightly higher register. The voice, I remember, seemed faintly
familiar. Even at the time, and as terrified as I was then, I realized
that this *There's no time for that* was a very strange thing to say. I
felt then an urge to physically confront this person, to run at him
and tackle him, even though I think I understood that I didn't
really understand what attacking him in that way would mean,
what consequences there might be, and this understanding meant
that I hesitated to do the thing my body seemed to want to do.
I'd been in only two fights in my entire life and hadn't fought well
either time—always, since I was old enough to remember, I'd been
the biggest, most physically imposing boy in any of the groups I'd

played with (though, no, there had been one boy who'd been taller than me whom I'd met on the first day of school at a school I later left long before the year was over, probably in part because of this boy, who, on that first day, had pushed me, hard, backwards over an exposed tree root, for really no reason, and the wind had been knocked out of me and I'd bruised my back and skinned both elbows, and always after I felt a deep hatred for this boy, and had, as a result, associated fighting, in part, with this boy and my deep hatred of him). Because I'd now spoken and no longer felt frozen in my spot at the end of the hall to the bedroom, I yelled out to my wife to call the police, and I'm not sure, now, whether this was the right thing to do—somehow I feel as though I shouldn't have dragged her into it, should have tried to protect her instead of asking her to protect me—but at the time, it didn't matter, because as soon as I'd started speaking, the person closed the refrigerator and walked further into the kitchen, toward what had once been the back door to the house but which, since the addition of the mother-in-law unit on the back where the Uber driver lived, had become a kind of uninsulated closet with our electrical panel and the hot water heater in it. He couldn't leave that way, I knew, and so the fact that he was going that way did not and could not remedy the situation; it seemed less like he was retreating or trying to get away than that he was completely ignoring me and doing whatever it was he'd come to do.

While I was mentally scanning the room for something to hit this man with, I realized I'd have to somehow keep him in the house until the police arrived or else get him to leave the house, and this, I remember, seemed unendurable; what I really wanted was for him never to have been there at all. I realized also that he could, of course, turn around at any time—he was on the other side of the kitchen island, out of sight from where I still stood at the end of the hallway to the bedroom—and, with only me to stop him, head toward the bedroom and my wife, who I'd inadvertently told him was there in the house. I could hear my wife speaking on the phone to the police, telling them what was happening and then giving them our address and asking when they would be here, could they get here soon?—neither one of us had forgotten how long it had taken before—and suddenly I remember thinking: Is that really our address? I couldn't, in that moment, remember our street address, or, rather, in that moment, I lost all confidence that the address I was then thinking of (the one my wife had, I thought, just spoken aloud) was in fact the address of the house I was standing in or one of the addresses we (my wife and I) had lived in since we'd begun living together ten years before, and what if she had it wrong and the police went to some other house down the block or even on the other side of the bayou?

The fact that I felt certain of what room the intruder was in was calming, was, in fact, the only thing, in that moment, that I felt entirely certain of, the one thing I felt I had some control over, even though of course his presence in the house was what made everything else so completely uncertain and frightening. And at precisely the moment I came to this realization, the man appeared on the other side of the living room, in front of the windows and nowhere near the kitchen, so that, at first, I thought this couldn't be the same man, and, before I could even register what had happened, he'd stabbed himself with our kitchen shears, once and then again, and again, in what I thought was his abdomen but turned out to be his upper thigh. I remember screaming when I'd first spotted him in a place I hadn't expected him to be, and I remember the man still standing or hunching over more or less calmly in front of the coffee table; now leaning down to put his hand on it, then slumping down a bit more and falling over in front of the couch, and then the smell of him reaching me suddenly, the smell of blood and something else, a repellent smell, and an odd kind of airborne warmth, too, a dizzying warmth all around me, like I was about to pass out.

As far as I know, this man died from his self-inflicted wound, or, rather, from the blood loss that it caused; the police, at first, couldn't be sure it was self-inflicted, and I'd had to go to the station, to make a statement, and I'd had to—in the middle of the night, at a time when there was no one to ask about how to do this properly, or what doing this properly even meant—find a lawyer, a lawyer we couldn't really afford but who, it was impressed upon me, was absolutely essential to the process, without whom the police didn't really feel comfortable asking me what had happened, what I'd seen, what I'd done. I'm sure it was obvious to the police that I was disturbed by what I'd seen, and I think—I half remember doing so—I think I started to tell them about the taller boy who'd pushed me over the tree root on the first day of school and my feeling of wanting to hurt this person who'd broken into our house in the middle of the night, and this made them think maybe I needed someone there who would do a better job of representing my best interests than I was then capable of (my wife had, apparently, emphasized that she didn't know who'd stabbed who, that, because she was in bed the whole time, she couldn't say for sure that I hadn't been the one who'd stabbed this man, she really only could say what she'd done, which had been to grab her Taser and her phone; she couldn't vouch for me at all). I remember drinking a Styrofoam cup of very dark coffee, so dark the taste of it lingered until I finally brushed my teeth, many hours later, not because I wanted it but because it was something to do while I waited, and I remember wondering where one even got Styrofoam cups anymore (weren't they bad for the environment? Now everyone used those thick paper ones, I thought), and I remember waiting for what seemed like days for anything at all to happen—no one asked me anything after it had been established that I needed a lawyer, and no one talked to me, and I wasn't sure if I could leave the room, so I didn't leave the room, not even to use the bathroom. Eventually, though, a woman showed up, looking very tired, and told me I could go home, and later I'd learn that this was the lawyer my wife had hired. My wife texted to say she was in the car in the parking lot, and then, as I walked all the way around the building looking for the car and the right parking lot—there were several parking lots, all with seven-foot high fencing around them, all otherwise identical, and my wife was driving the rental car, a car I still wasn't familiar with and that I found difficult to recognize even after weeks of her driving it—there were two follow-up texts asking where I was, were they holding me after all?, and then I finally found her and she told me the woman with the police scanner had posted that the man who'd stabbed himself was our catty-corner neighbor, the husband of the woman who was on trial for drowning her twins in the bathtub, and I realized then why his voice had been familiar to me.

When we got home, the police were still at the house. Just one police officer, in plainclothes but with a uniform vest, taking pictures of the walls and the floors in the house with a large camera with a very bright flash—we waited outside on the porch while he finished up, and afterwards asked if we could go back in, whether there was anything we should or shouldn't do. My wife also asked him about the coroner, whether there would be some sort of inquest. By then, and even as tired as I was, I'd started thinking differently about everything my wife or I said to the police, thinking that it all must seem at least somewhat suspicious in their eyes. Later, through the lawyer I never actually saw in person again, I learned that the police had believed my story and would probably have declined to bring charges even if they'd been suspicious of me, because of the state's so-called *stand your ground* law and because the man who'd been in our house—the catty-corner neighbor, a man who'd moved out even before his wife's arraignment, the woman with the police scanner posted, to move back in with his mother, who then died under suspicious circumstances, after which the man, this woman posted, was rumored to have lived in the homeless encampment on the other side of the railroad tracks, and then, eventually, moved back into his own house, though without removing the plywood on the doors and without moving in anything his brother had moved out when he left— clearly wasn't supposed to be in our house. (Also because, though this was never said aloud, the man was suspected in the murder of his mother and so his death wasn't an especially high priority for the police, and the police were overworked, and looked for any excuse not to pursue an investigation.)

Somehow the chair found out about all of this—maybe she, like my wife, followed the woman with the police scanner on social media—and called in the morning to tell me she was going to have my classes that afternoon covered and that I ought to meet with my lawyer and rest; these were the priorities she listed, and in that order: meet with my lawyer, then rest. I didn't have a story-lecture written for the final class later that week, and I realized that, if I didn't teach that day, I could just deliver the story-lecture I'd planned to deliver that day on the last day of class and then I wouldn't have to come up with something new for the last class, even though the story-lecture I'd planned to deliver that day wasn't really meant for the final day of classes and wouldn't do much to conclude the course.

While I scrubbed the floors and the coffee table and, after discovering a small hand print on the sofa, I turned the cushion over to hide it, and while my wife cleaned the kitchen and complained about the headache she had from not sleeping, the lawyer called to tell me I didn't have anything to worry about, and as far as I know, that's where the matter stands now. I've always been a little nervous about asking about the investigation into the neighbor who killed himself in our house, not wanting to call attention to myself as a possible subject of investigation. The thing I remember best about what happened after he stabbed himself was the smell, and that smell was why I was scrubbing the floors with the magic eraser and why my wife was telling me to use vinegar, and bleach, and hot water, and baking soda—natural things, she said, things that wouldn't make us sick.

On

His Son's Stuffed Animals,
One in Particular

But I think I started to tell the story about the break-in for some other reason, because of what the catty-corner neighbor did just before stabbing himself, I think. It was dark, as I've already said, and so I can't be completely sure, but I thought, at the time, that, when I'd first seen him in the kitchen, he'd been holding one of my son's stuffed animals, a stuffed animal my son had liked much more than his others, so much more than his other stuffed animals that he'd actually given the others names derived from its name, Hugbee—at first, I remember, he'd just used Hugbee as a name for *all* of his stuffed animals, and when he wanted one, he'd demand *Hugbee*, and my wife or I would go through the long process of going to his room, getting out the stool, reaching up to the animal boxes on the high shelves, and bringing down first one stuffed animal (usually the one that was the easiest to reach, or else, if we felt particularly insightful, as though we were really reading his mood that day, reaching past that one for another), and then, presenting this trophy to our son, watching his face crumple into tears of frustration as he shouted *Hugbee, Hugbee,* meaning, *No, not that one,* at which point we'd go back to the shelves and pull down another one, which, usually, also, would turn out to be the wrong one; in my memory, neither my wife nor I ever seemed to get it right before the third or fourth stuffed animal, and, though I would never say this to my wife or to anyone else, it sometimes seemed like our son didn't really have a set choice in mind when he asked for Hugbee, like what he'd really wanted was to have us go and get first one then another stuffed animal, and no matter what we returned with, to refuse it, and only settle for whatever stuffed animal came third or fourth, after we'd expended some real effort at pleasing him. In any case, after this period when he called all of his stuffed animals Hugbee, after that, he only called this one stuffed animal, his favorite, Hugbee, and the others had syllables added to them, like Kay-Hugbee and Nigh-Hugbee and See-Hugbee. Though these were, I think, somewhat fluid names, in the sense that sometimes Nigh-Hugbee was the lobster and sometimes it was the clam—both bought at an aquarium we'd visited over winter break—Hugbee, the one and only Hugbee, was always this vaguely bearish animal with a disturbingly human face, a toy neither my wife nor I could remember buying and that we therefore thought must have been a gift, though we never could agree on who exactly had gifted it to him. My son carried this Hugbee with him all the time, and his worst tantrums were reserved for those times when Hugbee couldn't be found or was being washed, and Hugbee was a sad, battered and worn toy, but I wouldn't have mistaken its outline in the neighbor's hand, and I didn't, I'm sure, mistake his gesture, offering me the toy from behind the refrigerator door. I didn't remember this, I should say, that night, either during questioning by the police or after, when I'd returned home and my wife, exhausted, had insisted we go through the whole house and see whether anything was missing. Hugbee—my son's Hugbee—ought to have occurred to me then, as something the catty-corner neighbor had without question at least taken brief possession of, but it didn't, not at that time, and, in any case, as we went through the kitchen cupboard by cupboard, we didn't find it. Sometime after dawn, after my wife had called in to work and the chair had called me, and when we were once again lying in our bed, not sleeping, Hugbee, clutched in the neighbor's hand, came suddenly and forcefully into mind, and I jumped up out of bed.

Hugbee was where I'd put him, alone on the worktable in the garage, the only one of my son's toys that I'd taken out of the box of his toys, as grimy and dirty with use as ever but not bloodied, definitely not bloodied. I picked him up and turned him over to reassure myself that this was the same stuffed animal, the same disturbingly human-looking bear, and it was. I remember I wondered if the memory I'd had was real, if I'd really seen the man offering Hugbee to me, but I remembered it so vividly in that moment that I decided it had to be, and, when she asked what I was doing and why I'd gone outside, and even though I knew she wouldn't want to hear it just then, I found myself telling my wife the story of Phrixus and his sister Helle, whose stepmother Ino had become jealous of Phrixus because he was her husband's, which is to say, his father's, favorite. Ino, I told my wife, wanted her own natural-born son to be named heir to the throne, and so she had her servants roast all of the village's seeds over a fire before they could be planted so that nothing in the fields would grow, and, when the villagers came to say that nothing grew no matter what they did, Ino bribed the men who were to be sent to the oracle to ask for relief from the gods with her body, telling these men that they should blame the famine on Phrixus when they spoke to the oracle. When this had been done and the villagers had been informed of what the oracle had said, a pyre was built at the altar of Zeus and Phrixus was carried up the mountain to it, and just as the priest was preparing to sacrifice Phrixus, his mother, Nephele, came down out of the sky riding a golden ram, and the ram took Phrixus out of the arms of the priest, and Helle, his sister, asked the ram to please not leave her behind, and so she was taken, too. Though I didn't get to say this, this ram was the same ram that Phrixus would later sacrifice to show his appreciation to the father of the gods, the same ram whose fleece would become the Golden Fleece, guarded by a sleepless dragon until Jason came to take it.

I didn't get to tell my wife any of this because, as soon as I'd mentioned the pyre and the sacrifice of Phrixus, she'd said *Just stop* and then rolled over on her other side and was asleep in moments, or at least she seemed to be asleep; she'd looked exhausted through the whole story, when she even bothered to open her eyes or face me, and I knew not to wake her after her reaction to my story, but

I stayed up, sweating through the midmorning, and eventually got out of bed and went into the dining room, where I sat at the table, looking out the window at birds coming and going in the camellia in the front yard. This seems strange to say, but all I could think about—all I remember thinking about, for what had seemed like hours—was my wife telling me to *Just stop*, the way she'd said it and my thoughts about why she might have said it and what might have happened if she'd listened all the way to the end; what I mean is that I didn't sit there thinking, not consciously, about the man who'd broken in or about my interview with the police or what my wife and I had had to clean up when we got back home. The whole horrible night I'd just been through wasn't first in my mind, although I can easily imagine that it, too, must have been somewhere in the background, a part of my distraction, but just a part, maybe not even a big part, but her reaction to my feelings or what I'd tried to express of those feelings was somehow more troubling to me, and now I see that in thinking that way, I was callously ignoring the fact that she, too, had been through those things—and others—and would naturally now, after all that happened, be very tired and probably also disturbed, and could want only to rest.

He Explains How He
Came to Have the Egg

I admit to struggling, for what must have seemed like forever to my wife, to find anything, really anything, with which to occupy myself after the accident—I even admitted it at the time, in my own way, though I don't (and didn't) believe that the fact that I recognized that I was struggling made that struggle any less difficult to deal with for either my wife or myself; if anything, I think, this willingness to attribute blame to myself really only made my malaise worse, because, once I'd recognized that my wife was healing in a way I wasn't, I started to think about ways to move on and realized that I would almost certainly *not* free myself from my malaise because after all I was the one who'd caused it, and so I remember I became despondent, and I sank deeper into this malaise. During this period—a period that stretched from the accident itself well over a year earlier to the time I'm now describing—I remember my wife first encouraging (at the suggestion of our social worker) and then finally demanding I find some kind of occupation for myself, some small side project to which to devote myself when I wasn't teaching (and teaching wasn't a distraction for me; if anything, it contributed to the malaise, in fact, because my experiments—the speech-acts-language, the agglutinative English, the story-lectures—were so obviously disasters, and because of my earlier loss of faith in my discipline), in order, at the very least, to pass the time, to occupy myself while this malaise worked itself out of my system, something mindless and tedious and above all time-consuming. (Because there was this thought then that it was simply a transitory state and not something I would continue to deal with for the remainder of my life, I think.) My wife, I guess, had already resigned herself to the idea that I wouldn't be re-dedicating myself to my job (my job, I think she must have known, was even then a lost cause, though I did go through the motions, and presented my changing speech patterns to her as exercises in pedagogy). She told me she couldn't relax while I was around, and what was I always sighing about, and, if I was going to be at home so often, maybe there were things around the house I could do, things I didn't deny I'd long put off, putting them off in the moment thinking I was, in doing so, only recognizing my own incompetence in such matters but then realizing later that putting these things off was really only a way to put off making the place we lived more comfortable and more permanent as a home, a tendency I eventually recognized as counterproductive to my own interests in maintaining the home we had—however precariously—already made. I was, by nature or by temperament, I think, not especially industrious—there had been that period of intense scholarship with which I'd begun my so-called *career*, before I'd even finished my dissertation, but when that hadn't produced much more than my instructorship, my productivity had tailed off rapidly—but I recognized that if I didn't at least *look* busy, things between my wife and me would get worse, or, really, since there must be a point at which things can't deteriorate any further, and because it seemed obvious to me, because of her remarks, that we must have already reached that point, a point at which that deterioration, the advanced state of it, I mean, has already begun to show, like the first wrinkles on the skin of the apple hinting that what lies underneath has already collapsed in on itself, and so, as a compromise, I started to at least *try* to learn how to replace electrical outlets, plug and caulk holes in the siding, fix the tiles on the kitchen counters, in short, to do all the things we'd asked our landlord to do but that he hadn't done. Though some of these projects necessitated that I take some part of the project with me into the garage—there was an old work table there that I could use, after I'd cleaned it off—still, it wasn't until the following summer, the period I've been describing, that I really started to spend any appreciable time there, and this, the fact of my spending more time there, ultimately had less to do with any specific home improvement project than it did with the state of the relationship between my wife and myself.

The garage, it should be said, wasn't a place either I or my wife really ever went prior to all this. It wasn't wide enough to house either one of our cars, really more of a longish shed, and, at some point, a work table had been installed at one end, along with a pegboard (although there were, when we moved in, no tools, or no working tools, in the garage, only boxes and boxes of papers and some landscaping equipment that wasn't working or else was never used), which cut down even further on the space inside. The garage was hot and humid, the conditions inside indistinguishable from those outside, and the fixture above the worktable worked only some of the time, and the place was usually filled with stinging and biting insects, and so, after the initial day or so of us poking around in all of the different corners of the place we'd just rented, there had been no real reason for us to go in.

Before I could make use of it, then, that April (even though it was technically spring, the first few major storms had already come ashore elsewhere in the state by then), my first job was to make it into a place I could stand being for any length of time, which required a great deal of work, but which work, I quickly discovered, I somehow perversely enjoyed. I think it was that I recognized that all of my labor in that area was only enforcing or creating a very temporary state, a state so fragile that, even if my vigilance in maintaining it were interrupted for, say, three days together, the garage would immediately fall back into ruin—the wet cardboard of the boxes would sprout from the floor, the walls and eaves would bloom again with wasps' nests, there would be animal tracks on the cement. The structure itself was sound, though there were very small gaps at the bottom of the drywall through which outside light and insects came that I filled with a very thick bead of caulk and the rest of the wood putty I found, having nothing better on hand and having no sense of good carpentry practices or the tools or materials to carry out anything more permanent or comprehensive. After I'd done that, I set off a bug bomb in the garage, an old one I'd found under the kitchen sink, a dud, I think, and then destroyed the three wasps' nests I found under the eaves outside with a broom, being careful to spray each one continuously with the bug spray for maybe a full minute or more, until it was all I could smell and I worried I would pass out. I also eventually carried out the old file boxes left there by our landlord; I'd hesitated for days, maybe as long as a week, to even open them because they looked darkened and wet and had clearly lost their structural integrity and I knew that once I started handling them, I would have to finish the job quickly, but I was sure they had millipedes or earwigs or other things in them, and they took up way too much space. They were, I discovered, filled with old receipts and tax documents, wetted and now mostly fused together, having turned a slightly bluish-white with polka dots of still-clear text, and the boxes themselves were impossible to handle as intended— once, they'd had handles carved out of their sides near the lid, but trying to pick them up by these handles only resulted in me tearing their tops off—and so I pushed them very slowly with my feet out to the curb in front of the next-door neighbor's house (the garage was closer to his house than to ours), reasoning, as I did so (though I recognized this reasoning as both cowardly and, ultimately, very silly), that I would, by putting them there, have established some sort of plausible deniability. It was there, by the next-door neighbor's trashcans, that I saw the egg that had once, and then only for a very short period of time, lain in the pine straw in the catty-corner neighbor's front bed, under their picture window, the dilapidated flesh-colored papier-mâché egg, now dented and much paler in color but, miraculously, still intact, and I felt, for reasons I didn't then entirely understand, that I couldn't leave it there, and so I brought it back to the garage, having nowhere else to put it.

I remembered arguing with my wife over whether it was fair to call the woman who'd lived in the house catty-corner to us with her husband and their twins an agoraphobe. This woman had been the subject of gossip in the neighborhood more or less since she'd moved in, and so, when the police came to dig up the bed underneath the picture window, the bed that had once had hostas in it, at least as far as I could remember, but then overnight whatever had been planted there disappeared and a big, ugly Easter egg was set in their place, the police had had to ask everyone to please go back inside, to stop crowding around, to let the detectives do their work. We—my wife and I; our son must have been napping—watched from our front window. One of the men brought up one and then two bags out of the hole and, although I know this will only make me seem even more depraved—it's precisely that this all makes me seem so much more depraved that, I feel certain, is what brings it to mind in the first place—I can remember, in that instant, seeing those bags and feeling the shock and horror anyone, I thought, would feel at seeing such a thing but then immediately and as though seeking relief in the memory, thinking back to this argument we—my wife and I—had once had, me telling my wife as though it was a thing she would have forgotten that when our son was an infant—and, obviously, this had been at a time when it was still possible to speak of our son in this kind of offhand way, a time, in other words, when our son was still alive—we'd rarely left the house; maybe, I'd said, this woman just didn't want to wake the babies, or was feeding, or maybe, I'd thought but didn't say, maybe she was just agoraphobic. I had, I realize now, even then a tendency to disagree with my wife almost as though by reflex, and I sometimes found myself saying things I didn't believe and couldn't pretend to believe long enough even to get through what I was saying. Why was it so important to me that she be wrong? she asked. I had no answer. I can only say that it didn't seem right to me, in that moment, holding the egg, to treat it like garbage, to erase or discard a kind of monument or token of a family's history, and so I rescued it.

In Which

Something Is Dislodged

When I then returned to the garage with the egg, I discovered I hadn't rid the garage of all its insects, or anyway hadn't rid it of all the evidence of insects, because I could now see, behind where the stack of file boxes had been and in the corner next to the far edge of the pegboard, one large insect nest or hive near the ceiling. Though it seemed much too muted in its color to be something living, still, it had a strange kind of dull iridescence and didn't look like any nest or hive I'd ever seen, seeming, at first glance, to be the general shape of a moth but much larger. Whatever it was, I remember that it terrified me; I dropped the egg on the hard concrete and backed somewhat clumsily out of the garage. I'd never been brave when it came to wild animals and pests, had even crossed the street when my wife stopped to look at a stray dog's collar, and I'd only cleared out the wasps' nests through the most overpowering boredom and discomfort—I knew I couldn't be inside the house, but I knew I would never go in the garage unless the nests were gone. I didn't close the door to the garage, hoping, I think, that whatever this thing was, it would decide to leave on its own, and it took me maybe a full hour of vacillating to force myself to go back into the garage and then get close enough to see that what I was looking at was neither a hive nor a nest, in that it didn't contain a living insect but was instead more in the nature of a snake's skin, something lacking the substance of the insect it had once housed but otherwise identical to that insect's outward appearance. This thing affixed to the wall where it met the ceiling seemed as though it had only recently been shed and was now starting to dry, the way glue or oatmeal forms a skin upon contact with the air that one knows one can disturb readily and without much force. I was, I remember, briefly and for reasons that, at the time, I couldn't quite connect to what I was seeing, reminded of a cat that had crawled into my father's tools (my father wasn't, in any sense, handy, and almost never fixed anything himself, but, mysteriously, he did have a number of tools that all showed a great deal of use) in our garage when I was maybe twelve or thirteen, a cat that didn't belong to us—though it did, afterwards, become *our cat*—and that then gave birth to kittens.

When I reached out to try to remove this whatever this was from the wall, I thought I saw the thing that must have created it or extruded it still inside, pulsing or breathing or working in what was to me an extremely repulsive way, though now I think this can only have been an illusion, and I'm not ashamed to say that I probably shrieked, I think probably very loudly, and ran out of the garage yet again, knocking over a rusting aluminum watering can left there by our landlord and also tripping over the end of the broom I'd brought out to the garage to dislodge the wasps' nests from under the eaves. The watering can fell to the concrete in the garage, also very loud, ringing when it first collided and then making a strangely echoey sound as it rolled on the garage floor, like someone sawing wood in the far distance.

This—most definitively that moment—was when I felt the strain in the relationship between my wife and myself most strongly, by which I mean that I couldn't imagine doing anything at all in that moment except to go to my wife and tell her what I'd seen and show her my skinned and bruised knee, as if to share this was also to take away at least some small part of its power to frighten me, and even maybe to insist she come with me to see the thing in the garage, too, so that I could show her I was frightened of something worth being frightened of, or so that her reaction would give my own a kind of scale, as when a ruler or a coin is put beside something small in a photograph, so that my own reaction wouldn't seem so ridiculous—and all of this was transparently self-serving, since I was the only person who knew what my reaction had been, or that I'd even had a reaction. But as soon as I'd grabbed the handle of the door that led inside from the porch, I realized, given our current situation, I couldn't possibly tell her what I'd seen. I mean that I could already guess what her reaction would be—she would be or would make herself seem bored by it, because, I thought, she had, at that time, decided that most of what I did, maybe even *all* of what I did, was really of no concern to her. I knew she would give me not even half her attention, and, like someone hearing only one person's part of a conversation between three people, would come away thinking that not much had been said, and that what had been said was, honestly, uninteresting. My adrenaline in that moment, though, was such that I might still have told her if I hadn't heard her on the phone when I walked through the door. I knew that if I interrupted the call, and even though it would seem, momentarily, like I had her attention, really she would be just as distracted as ever, only then she would be distracted by thoughts of how rude I'd been to interrupt her conversation, and by her memories of the many times I'd interrupted conversations she was having or did something that showed her how little respect I had for her and for the person she was talking to; I had no idea how many, and even *that* would become something with which she could attack me, because it would show, really once and for all, that I hadn't been paying attention (she loved to turn my complaints around and use them against me), that *I* was the one who was distracted—distracted by thoughts of myself—and not committed to the relationship anymore, not she. She could have been on the phone with someone important, doing something important, after all, and what did I want to talk to her about? Why was I butting in? A bug? A bug's nest? What was the matter with me? In short, I opened the door, took one step into the house, heard her talking on the phone in the bedroom, and stopped dead in my tracks, thinking: Who can I tell if I can't tell my wife? What can I do with this information that there's a giant bug in the garage in some strange nest?

The only thing I could think to do was to take the broom I'd left outside and use it to poke the nest or whatever it was in the garage. Given the size of the thing I'd seen, I later thought, this idea could only have been the result of my feeling of desperation, of my fear, and the adrenaline my body had released (probably, also, my lack of sleep, and the general disorderedness of my mind that day). I felt, I remember, like I was bouncing while walking, and I had to struggle to keep myself quiet, and when I reached out for the broom I'd knocked over, I stupidly jammed one of my fingers on the doorframe. That was when I heard the humming. Though it really looked very little like the one I'd seen on campus—this one was more recognizably an insect, with a strange brownish-green color that was much too shiny and slick to have been feathered, I thought; it looked almost like it had been slathered in Vaseline, in fact—still, because of its size and because of the way it moved, I recognized it as probably the same thing I'd seen on the roof in the net of the man I'd later discovered was an entomologist. Like the one that had attacked my office window, this one moved erratically but quite fast, so that I couldn't get a good sense of what it looked like, and I'm left with this vague impression of a very chunky hummingbird with long legs.

(It occurs to me now that the fact that we usually think of the image of a thing at rest as the best and most accurate representation of that thing, even when, as in the case of all living things *by definition*, the thing in question is never actually completely at rest—and, in the case of some living things, like hummingbirds or sharks, is almost never even perceptibly still—is strange. I mean that I guess that, when I thought about it, I felt that this preference in representation for the lifeless didn't make sense, or else—and this was, to me, a more disturbing possibility—that preference is revealing of the way we see other living things. I was thinking, specifically, about the picture of the hummingbird I'd seen in an encyclopedia when I was much younger—seeing this picture of a hummingbird, I remember I'd had an idea of the animal itself, a smaller bird than the parakeets my brother had had, but otherwise not especially beautiful (why was my father so interested in them, I'd wondered), but when we vacationed in Colorado one summer and these things suddenly appeared on the back porch of the cabin we were staying in and my father got so excited about these strange, at times disturbing, sounds that made my eardrums flutter, I couldn't reconcile the image I'd long had of the thing and this specific appearance of the thing. I guess what I really mean is that it seems strange that we consider the true picture of a creature not to be that creature in action (especially when those actions are what define our relationship with that animal; mosquitoes bite us, for instance, horses pull things for us, bears stand on their hind legs to threaten us, and so on) but instead its opposite, its dead body, or else its body as it will look only in death, and only truly under ideal conditions and even then for a very limited period of time. It's not that I don't realize still images are better than nothing, just that it seems at least a little strange that we would ever have thought of still images as sufficient, as though we'd been trying to capture a smell with a drawing or a sound through cooking. Anyway, it would be naïve, I think, to say that this line of thinking doesn't have anything to do with the dog we saw on our way to the Macy's, or I suppose, with other things, about which I can't speak.)

I was, at the time, very conscious—though I should be careful to say I only mean I was, I think, especially conscious of *this way of thinking*, or else this way of thinking was particularly strong, at the time, or else even that I was really only more *aware* of this way of thinking's recurrence at the time; I don't mean, that is to say, that this way of thinking was itself unprecedented, or that it hasn't since recurred, or that I had, at the time, only recently become aware of it—of the possibility that this thing might injure me, by which I mean I actively imagined the consequences of such an injury. At the time, I remember, I thought about the consequences of serious injury so often, in fact, that such thoughts had become for me a dangerous preoccupation, and so themselves increased the likelihood of serious injury—I had trouble focusing on the road while driving, for instance, looking constantly in the side-view and rearview mirrors and sometimes, as a result, forgetting to look through the windshield in front of me, and I'd cut my finger while dicing an onion because I was worried about cutting my finger and was trying to hold the onion the way I knew I was supposed to but had never held an onion while dicing it, and I'd nearly fallen many times because I was worried about tripping over things that weren't there or weren't actually tripping hazards—and so I'd begun to think that I ought to try to change my way of thinking altogether. I often found myself thinking gruesomely morbid thoughts, and when, as though on their own, hints of these thoughts slipped out in conversation with my wife, she looked at me as though what I was saying wasn't just ridiculous but also very likely a sign of a serious mental issue needing the immediate attention of professionals. I can remember thinking, for instance, while standing in the shower, not that I might slip and fall, hitting my head and possibly suffering brain damage such that I stopped breathing and died—though I was, I think, conscious that such things did happen to otherwise healthy people—but that I was glad I'd gone to the bathroom before getting into the shower because, *if* I were to slip and fall and hit my head, my thought was that I might immediately lose control of my bowels, and that it was bad enough that I would be discovered naked—which is to say that I would be made even more vulnerable and defenseless by the condition in which I was found—but that my condition would be, besides extraordinarily vulnerable, also incredibly embarrassing, and that my wife, finding me in such a situation, might be at least a little more reluctant to help—I thought *I* would be, in her situation. I mean, I think, that I'd become more conscious of the sometimes-hidden consequences of serious injury. A reasonable question (or anyway a question that I remember seemed reasonable to me at the time) was: If I became incapacitated by such a fall—and I would have to be incapacitated if I involuntarily urinated or defecated, and though I knew that after death people defecated, now I wondered whether they also urinated, though I wasn't curious enough to look it up or ask someone who might have known—my concerns would neither be that

I'd urinated or defecated nor that I might be embarrassed by the fact of my having urinated or defecated, but would be concerned only with my survival, wouldn't they? Could my embarrassment at my involuntary reaction to my serious injury cause a significant delay in my recovery? Weren't there seemingly always stories in the news of horribly naïve people experiencing miraculous recoveries after serious injuries because of optimism that, given the severity of their injuries, was at the very least misplaced if not itself dangerous in most other contexts? Wasn't it at least possible, I thought, that the opposite would hold true, too, that those who despaired of recovery would find it always just out of reach? When I mentioned—as though without properly thinking through the consequences of speaking this aloud, as though without considering whether it was a thing my wife would be interested in—that I always used the bathroom before I showered, my wife gave me the look she gave me when I'd told our son some obvious untruth in her presence, and then, when I explained that I didn't want her to find me on the floor of the shower having shit all over myself after I'd slipped and hit my head, she looked very concerned.

But I was trying to explain something else, something about the insect and the thing it had left in the garage. In the moment and immediately after it had flown away, I worried that there might be another insect around—I didn't yet know for certain the thing in the garage definitely *wasn't* a nest or hive—despite the obvious fact that the insect flying in front of me a few moments before had seemed *larger* than the thing I'd found in the garage, had even seemed as though it couldn't possibly have fit itself into such a relatively small space, but then I remembered I'd always thought the same about the wasps that came pouring out of wasps' nests, so I didn't consider it impossible that other such insects might be inside the remnant or whatever it was I'd found on the wall of the garage. To be safe, I prodded this remnant with the handle of the broom—though the bristle end was difficult to hold, it seemed like the wrong tool for the job, by which I mean I didn't feel I could learn anything by brushing the remnant with the bristles of the broom; instead, I felt that it was more likely I would only destroy the thing with the bristles, and so, after I'd looked on the porch for a better option—the grill, the chimney starter, a half-rotted bag of charcoal briquets, a citronella candle, a long-handled lighter for the grill that was probably out of butane and had been out in the rain anyway—and still came up empty, I decided to hold onto the bristles and prod the remnant with the handle of the broom.

The remnant, I found, was very firm, like a thin layer of hard plastic, and, when I knocked it lightly with the handle, nothing came out. I got a little closer—I'd been as far away as the broom would allow me to be—and then, after I'd hit the thing a little harder and still nothing happened, I got a little closer again. Though I couldn't tell from which end or from where the insect had first emerged, I decided to crouch down—something about being low to the ground then appealed to me, I think, like it made me safer—and look up into it, and it was from that angle that I discovered a small hole; small, though big enough to admit the end of the broom handle, which I of course (and I know this seems very Freudian) then put into the hole. With very little pressure, the remnant came off the wall, peeling away almost at once, but now it adhered to the end of the broom handle, like when you try to shake a dead cockroach out of the paper towel you've used to pick it up off the floor and can't dislodge it.

Naturally, and despite all I'd been thinking just moments before, my first instinct was to take the broom and the remnant on the end of it inside to show my wife what had been in the garage, but before I'd even stepped onto the porch, I realized I would still not be welcome there, and so I stopped, turned around, and, unsure of what to do, walked back to the garage and then paced in a circle in front of the door. My wife, I knew, wouldn't be interested in this thing; she would ask why I'd brought it into the house, and why couldn't I have just told her what it was and gotten rid of it like a normal person would have, or else she would act as though I didn't exist, as she had been doing—I would come in, say *Look what was in the garage*, and she wouldn't reply, and would get up and go to the bathroom if she heard me entering the kitchen—and, if I wouldn't leave her alone, she would still refuse to look at the thing and meanwhile find something about what I'd done to criticize: It's getting on the carpet, your shoes are dirty, you're going to knock something over with that broom—she wouldn't have had to look far, and I could have suggested many things myself, and she was twice as inventive as I was when it came to finding and exposing my faults. And so I stood there with this remnant on the end of the broom I held at arm's length, unable to decide what to do next, thinking that I couldn't go into the house, where my wife waited, and I thought, only very briefly and as though unconsciously, that I ought to feel guilty about the way I was thinking about her, assuming the worst, but in fact I felt no such guilt, I even blamed my wife for acting the way she'd been acting, rather than, as I thought I'd been doing, trying to find some sort of compromise, not yet realizing that, by staying in the house with me, by not explicitly blaming me for our situation, for my part in the matter we hadn't discussed and wouldn't discuss for some time, she was not only compromising but in fact being very kind to me, kinder than I deserved. She is, in general and in nearly every situation and for as long as I've known her, a person who looks for the best in others and often finds it, and so when she doesn't find it, that person must, I think, seem truly monstrous to her—was I such a person now?—while I, for my part, have long believed that few people are genuinely good, and so when I find such a person, as I found her, it seems miraculous, but still the baseness of other people just seems normal and so when people are depraved or the things they think and say are depraved, I'm never disappointed by it, or else when people are depraved or the things they think and say are depraved, I'm *always* disappointed by it, but never because I'm surprised they've acted that way, while for her, it must be a surprise, this depraved way I was acting and the depraved things I was saying, and, I think now, that might explain why her reactions to my actions and my words were as violently negative as they seemed to me then.

He Describes an Incident, Deeply Disturbing

I remember I eventually had to just leave the broom on the ground next to the garage because the remnant and what it had held reminded me of the incident on the roof, which reminded me of the entomologist, which reminded me of the weird hearing he'd chaired, which reminded me that, even though the chair had arranged to have my classes covered that day, I nevertheless had to go to campus. This was the way my brain worked then; I'd forgotten about the other hearing whose date had, after a long period of delay, finally been set the week before all of this until there I was, holding the broom and trying to decide to show my wife what I'd found and it was almost time for that hearing, and then, because I hadn't remembered it before, I worried I had the day wrong, and had to check my calendar. I can remember rushing through a very cold shower in the dark bathroom (I didn't even get all of the soap off my skin) and forgetting my belt, so that I couldn't tuck in my shirt, which was, I remember, dirty, stained near one of the cuffs and also down near my beltline, though I didn't notice this until I'd already arrived on campus.

The administration had tried to hide the true purpose of the hearing from the *larger campus community*, from, that is to say, the student representatives who would be serving on the panel; no text alert had been sent out advising students, faculty, and staff that an assault had happened on campus, though this was only what was called for under university bylaws, and there had been no advisory posts about the panel's hearing, either, though this, too, was called for. I might have been the only person attending this hearing who knew what had happened and why we were meeting and who was not part of the administration, and I still couldn't quite believe the administration had decided on this particular course of action, and as a result, I found myself doubting whether the meeting was actually being held for the reasons it was, I knew, being held; there was a thought, in the back of my mind, that somehow *I* was going to be punished for my role in all of this, for my failure to act.

Ultimately, I think it was probably the cowardice and greed of certain members of the administration that had made the hearing necessary in the first place—I mean that it was obvious the student should have been turned over to the police immediately, and it was equally obvious that neither I nor really any member of the faculty or the student body should have been given the responsibility of deciding a punishment for the actions of this student, and yet that was the situation, and anyway the conclusions were, it seemed, foregone, because the *charged party* had, long ago, left the country (I would, later, wonder whether the administration had helped, or at least warned the student that this was the best thing to do under the circumstances; it was a matter involving money, I thought, and so they could be counted upon to have done the most unethical thing possible), and with the victim still recovering in the hospital, maybe even as the panel was convening finally breaking through the haze of painkillers and learning that her face would be permanently scarred and puckered in certain places, even after the grafts, that there really was no going back to what her life had been like before—certainly, there hadn't been any such hearing that I knew of in my time at the university, and I'd never heard of such a thing happening before elsewhere, either, and besides, common sense (and sober legal counsel) would, I'm sure, have advised against holding such a hearing for any number of reasons of liability, but common sense, I knew, wasn't the administration's strength and cowardice, and, to a lesser degree, greed, was.

The incident had happened weeks before, and at a particularly difficult time; not only was it the middle of the semester, when I had a great deal of grading to do in addition to all of the work I had yet to do in preparing and planning the following weeks' classes, but it was also during the time when my wife and I were finally packing up our son's room, meaning, I thought, that we were, finally, trying to put the fact of his death behind us for good—not, I mean, that we were trying to forget him, only that we were hoping to remember him as he'd lived and hoping also to stop thinking so obsessively about the manner and nature of his death. (And later, now, I would realize that when I thought in terms of *we*, I really ought to have seen that I was only actually thinking about *me*, and that I should have seen this—my wife's insistence that we pack up our son's things and get rid of as much as we could—as an indication that everything between us was coming to an end after all, and that, after his room had been cleaned out, she would have almost nothing holding her there anymore.)

I'd reported the incident with the student immediately, by which I mean I had, for the first and only time, picked up the phone in the classroom during class and asked the operator to direct my call to campus police; had then described the horrible injury to the woman on the other end, trying my best to control my fear so that I could describe the incident that had caused it in as much detail as possible while also asking what on earth I was supposed to do for the student who'd had the acid splashed in her face, what I *could* do for that student; giving the attacker's name and, after some fumbling with my forgotten passwords and the classroom's computer, giving his student number; punctuating all of this with what I recognized were largely impotent requests for help, requests that were, really, requests that I be absolved of my responsibility, including any responsibility for the student's pain. An ambulance had to be called, of course, and I'd had to stay behind in the classroom to wait for the ambulance with the student and the two other students who had also been splashed with whatever the student had thrown and suffered minor injuries, and of course these students' friends, several of whom seemed to want to take charge of the situation and others of whom obviously wanted only to leave the room but who also seemed to feel guilty about wanting to leave the room, and so there was a crowd of people comforting each other standing apart from the victims who were crying hysterically except for the one who'd had the acid thrown in her face, who was quiet, probably from shock, and who I'd tried to help by pouring the rest of my water over her face, not knowing what else to do, and later I would wonder what I would have done if the attack had happened in my early class, when the mug would have been filled with hot coffee instead of water from the water fountain outside.

I'd had to miss my next class, and I'd had to explain to the class that would have met in the room after my class had finished that they couldn't come into the classroom, and I'd had to tell the professor of that next class that her class would have to meet elsewhere, just for today, even though everyone could hear the sound of the students crying through the closed door and everyone, I'm sure, could guess that something had gone horribly wrong, and I'm equally sure that the students who'd left had told everyone they met what had happened. Though the ambulance and the campus police finally arrived just after the next period began, still no one from the administration came, and, because there would have been no way for anyone in the administration to contact me unless they came to the classroom, I really had no idea whether they even knew what had happened, whether they knew that anything at all had happened, whether they had any sort of plan for what to do in such a situation, whether I was somehow legally or morally culpable for what had happened, or whether I was making a mistake in what I was then doing (though really in the moment all I could think was that I wanted my students to get to the hospital and receive medical treatment right away). Neither the attacker nor the victim had been exceptionally good students, though I think it bears saying that the attacker had been a particularly weak student and the victim was merely an indifferent, or seemingly indifferent, student, and although I didn't think these things at the time, what I thought instead was or seemed to be an attempt on my part to assuage my own guilt. The attacker had, clearly, done something reprehensible, but there was no way I could have foreseen such a bizarre act. Though I'd put the two students together in a group, and though I'd delivered what I hoped would be an intellectually provocative story-lecture (but not, I thought, one that might cause problems for the administration down the road, or for myself, with the administration; it was, after all, a story everyone already knew and that was taught in many classes at both high schools and universities), I couldn't know that something had passed between these two students that had stirred up such extreme emotions in the attacker. I couldn't know, for instance, whether the one had spurned the other at some late-night party, or whether the one had insulted the other on social media, or to her friends, or whether the attacker was going through the stress of being far away from home for the first time (he was an international student) and being asked to take on a great deal of responsibility, perhaps the first such responsibility he'd ever been asked to take on. None of these thoughts consoled me in the least, either at the time of the at-tack or after, but they all occurred to me, and I wondered whether this was the influence of the culture or, as ever, whether there was something innately duplicitous about the way our brains worked, always crafting stories to explain away the horrible things we did and said. The attacker threw the acid at a moment I wasn't looking at the students—I was scanning ahead in my notes to see what exactly I planned to do after their group discussions, though really I was thinking about what I could save of my son's things and where I could hide those things I couldn't save—and had already left the room by the time I registered that anything had happened, and I remember that the other members of that group of students had all pushed away from the student who'd had the acid thrown in her face, and that the sounds of desks falling over were my first indications something had gone wrong, and when I located the site of these sounds, the student's shirt seemed to be melting down from her shoulders and another student, the tall red-headed one with the wispy beard, got up, dry heaved, and left after he'd said this, said, *Don't let her touch her face; she'll mess up her hands, too.*

I'd told the students a version of the story of Shelley's *Frankenstein*, focusing on the creature, of course, though largely dismissing the many passages in which the creature is educated or in which characters speak to each other and instead spending most of my time describing, speculatively, Frankenstein's work in assembling the creature (which—and this has always struck me as odd and a serious flaw in the novel—in the novel, only takes up two pages) and the creature's anger at the fate Frankenstein designed for it (which also, strangely, is barely mentioned in the novel; instead, the creature mostly complains that it's alone, and that Frankenstein won't accede to its demands that he create a companion for it). I remember that I wanted to tell this story because I wondered whether Frankenstein could have been said to have *intended* the creature to suffer in some way—the usual interpretation of the story was that it was a kind of incompetence that had made Frankenstein's work clumsy (as well as, of course, the fact that what he was attempting to do was something that was really beyond the power of a single human being to effect, i.e., the creation of life), but this was *Frankenstein's* theory of the case, and therefore a distortion of the truth, and what if what the creature and others saw as hideous and cruel was actually, for Frankenstein, at least in its conception, beautiful? Because Frankenstein is the first to conclude that the creature is hideous (he's also the most insistent), it wasn't that I meant that he conceived of something beautiful but made something hideous; no, what I meant was that, because, at some level, he always intended the creature to have a miserable life, a life of anguish and loneliness, and because he saw he'd accomplished that goal, the creature was, or could have been, to him, beautiful as well as hideous. Naturally, such a reading made Frankenstein out to be even crueler than Shelley had written him, but then, I remember thinking my students would understand, wasn't this the point? Earlier in the semester, I'd told them the story of Yahweh expelling

Adam and Eve from the Garden, told them, I mean, that their punishment wasn't simply banishment from the Garden but in fact that Adam, besides being banished, had been told he now had, forever, the task of tilling fields of brambles and thistles, and Eve, from that point on, would have to endure the pain of childbirth (her first pregnancies ended, both times, in twins, I reminded my students, and these were natural childbirths—no epidurals), and when the two, despairing of their fate and what they'd lost, committed suicide by first starving themselves, then drowning themselves, then falling from a great height, Yahweh raised them from the dead each time, and this Yahweh, I said, was the same Yahweh who'd made the Tree of the Knowledge of Good and Evil in the first place (for what purpose if not to tempt Adam and Eve?), not to mention the serpent, and even the angel Satan, in order, one can only assume, to produce exactly that result.

That the administration would craft their own story about the assault and attempt to treat the whole incident as if it were something the university could—*should*—handle by itself was simultaneously unsurprising and yet still unthinkable, since, after all, one only read about universities attempting to handle serious crimes as matters of school business when those universities *failed* to protect either themselves or their students, failed also in keeping the incidents in-house and on-campus, had, in fact, in the end and through their own actions, opened themselves up, as institutions, to punishments and settlements from outside parties that, had these universities simply reported the incidents to the proper authorities when they occurred, would not, and indeed *could not* be considered fair or even necessary, because, after all, it wasn't the university that had been in the wrong in these incidents, not any more than a city could be considered liable for an explosion that destroyed almost an entire block next to a daycare center and a hospital simply because someone had set off a truck bomb that exploded in the middle of the downtown on a weekday, or for a series of disturbing break-ins merely because those break-ins took place in one of its neighborhoods, or for the myriad assaults and murders that happened because those assaults and murders had occurred within the city limits, and really the university ought to have known better, ought to have known covering up something like this wouldn't work, even though the reasons for trying to cover it up were obvious.

In this particular case, in the email I was sent, it was said that, in order to *provide students with a sense of security*—and, it went without saying, to protect those affected from outside scrutiny—I should exercise extreme discretion, by which it was meant that I shouldn't speak of the incident with anyone at all, not anyone outside of the administration itself, not even with the students affected or with the class, though I could scarcely prevent the class from bringing it up the next time we met, and the aftereffects of it never really went away; not only did the four students directly involved not re-join us, but other students, more than was usual, simply stopped coming to class. Though the campus police had been brought in, and though the campus police chief had, reportedly, advised the Dean of Students that the matter needed to be handed over to the proper authorities, the Dean of Students didn't take such action. It was said—the chair, anyway, said, because she'd been informed about the situation and forced me to sit in a meeting with her in which she gossiped for thirty minutes about the dean of the college and the Dean of Students and then finally let me go back to preparing for class—that the Dean of Students had been acting out of character, though really his actions seemed perfectly *in* character with what I knew of the administration and their cowardice, and so, when he directed the disciplinary committee to take up the issue, even the Dean of Students's subordinates thought, surely, something must have been miscommunicated. The office wouldn't confirm the panel's meeting time or where it would take place because, they said, no such meeting *should* be necessary—this was what they emphasized when I spoke to them, that such a meeting *shouldn't* be necessary, as though this meant that it hadn't already been called—and this naturally created a great deal of entirely unnecessary confusion.

In Which

He Explains What Happened at the Hearing, or, Really, What Happened Instead of the Hearing

Although the Dean of Students's office was directly across a grassy area from the library—not really a *quad*, since this grassy area was still mostly undeveloped and ignored by the campus's landscapers (maybe because the hedges that sprouted up here and there on its uneven slopes made it impossible to mow with their riding mowers)—it wasn't as though the two buildings were close to each other. The library was, in fact, a six- or seven-minute walk from the Dean of Students's office, and the paths leading to it were all indirect, detouring around other buildings or the newly fenced construction zone to the west (yet more business classrooms and a new parking lot, it was said), and anyway this pseudo-quad, such as it was, was on the side of the library that didn't face the student union, and so the sound, when it first occurred, was muffled by the library and by the distance—muffled also by the cinder-block construction of the Dean of Students's office and the thickness of the windows. I don't think I thought much about the sound the first few times I heard it, though it may only be that I didn't *want* to think much about the sound at the time, meaning I really didn't want to get involved in something just then, *another* something, not when there was already so much happening (*to me*, I inevitably thought, the ugly and unavoidable solipsism of which thought I even then immediately regretted).

It wasn't until the sound had repeated itself a number of times with a growing intensity and someone ran past the window outside, very fast, that the other faculty member in the waiting room—not someone I knew personally, but someone whose pompadour and thick acetate glasses I'd recognized from a convocation or *Celebration of Our Stellar Faculty* or some other not-explicitly-mandatory-but-nevertheless-actually-mandatory event—swivelled around in his chair and then we both got up, more or less at the same time, moving towards the windows on the opposite side of the room, from where we could just barely see a crowd of people crouching behind the dumpster enclosure beside the bus stop. His cell phone made some noise (mine buzzed in my pocket), and when it became clear that this noise wouldn't relent until he'd checked his phone, we both took our phones out and saw the *ALERT* message on our lockscreens telling us and all other campus personnel that there was an *active shooter situation*, and that we were now supposed to shelter in place and follow protocol. It was, I thought later, a good thing I hadn't been teaching that day, not only because I would have had to walk past the library to get to the Dean of Students's office from my classrooms, but also because I couldn't remember which version of the protocol I was supposed to be following, and so, when the shooting began, I would have been in the classroom or on my way out of it, to the Dean of Students's office where I now was, completely unprepared to deal with what was then happening. The only thing I could remember from the meeting with the chair at the beginning of the year was that I was supposed to attack the shooter if he (or she, or they, though it was always assumed it would be a he, and really everyone agreed that it would be a he and not a she or a they, since it was always, everywhere, a he) tried to enter the classroom. *With what* was never made clear, and I guessed that it was almost entirely due to my sense of outrage at being asked to attack anyone at all for any reason that I remembered this detail from that meeting. I thought, probably, that the protocol required me to lock the classroom doors, though maybe not, maybe that had been the old protocol, and anyway I couldn't recall a latch or a bolt on any of the doors to the classrooms I taught in (and there were, in all but one of those classrooms, also those emergency-exit-type doors to the outside, the ones with the bars running across them instead of a handle, and I didn't know how to lock such doors, or even *if* they could be locked manually or if it mattered), and I also thought the protocol also probably required me to remain out of sight and to advise my students to remain out of sight, though I wasn't sure how that would fit with the idea of me attacking the shooter (which, again, was the only detail I remembered clearly), and fortunately, all of my speculation about the protocol was moot because, under the circumstances, I wasn't in class and so I could just follow this other faculty member's lead (though, in that moment, he seemed just as confused as I was, and both of us simply stood there, looking out of the window, trying to figure out where this *active shooter* was).

I'd heard the earlier announcements over the loudspeakers—loudspeakers that, to that point, I hadn't known *were* loudspeakers; they only ever sounded digital chimes at noon and there had never been any such announcement before, not when I'd been on campus—but because we were so far away from the library where these loudspeakers were hung, the sound of the announcements had really been nothing more than a low but persistent mumble, identifiable as some sort of speech but nothing anyone in the Dean of Students's building could possibly understand and whose source was, at least when I first heard the sound of them, a mystery. What I thought was stranger was that no one in the building had said anything, not the student who'd sat at the reception desk, not any of the administrators whose doors, a moment ago, had been open, and not the Dean himself, who, I thought, given the hour and the nature of the meeting to come, should have already come out of his office at the far end of the hall off the waiting room to explain what exactly I was here to do. The faculty member who'd been waiting in the waiting room with me put his ear to the window and, without me asking, started to repeat what these announcements were saying: *If you have been shot, call 911. If you have not been shot, do not call 911 from your cell phone. If you see someone who has been shot, call 911.* This announcement had been repeating itself over and over since, I thought, the first of the muffled noises I now realized were gunshots, but I wasn't sure. It sounded like it was saying the same thing again, but then the faculty member with me repeated it: *Stay indoors. If you have been shot, call 911 from your cell phone.* I think it was the first part, the *Stay indoors,* that most disturbed me.

I remembered wondering if I was too close to the window; I told the faculty member that he shouldn't be where he was in front of the window. Eventually, though, this became unbearable—away from the window, we couldn't see what was happening, and we couldn't hear the announcements, either—and we both returned to the window but a step back and to the side from where we'd just been. From my side of the window, I could see what I at first believed to be a backpack but which, after looking at it a little longer, I realized must be a person *with* a backpack lying in the grass near the far end of the pseudo-quad, and I later learned that she—because it *was* a person, a student—was probably already dead by the time I saw her, having bled out from three gunshot wounds, and I also saw—though from very far away and through a stand of trees—someone else actually get shot leaving one of the frat huts near the library, though, from that distance and with the trees in the way, it would be more correct to say I saw what I thought was a person fall and then, a fraction of a second later, heard a shot, with the delay in the sound reaching me making it seem as though the two things were related only coincidentally.

I've since been told that a paper the entomologist wrote on the psychotropic effects of the song of a species of Amazonian cicada, *Quesada tristeza,* had been sent back the day before the shooting with a note that accused him, more or less, of fabricating, in their entirety, his results, and I was told also that really, at that time, very few people had even accepted the existence of *Q. tristeza* as a species distinct from *Q. gigas,* the so-called Giant Cicada, though I should say that most of what I know about the situation is what I learned later and basically by accident, from our gossipy chair, who didn't like me but did like talking, and who'd requested the meeting, as I'd only learn at the end of the meeting, to inform me that my position was ending and my contract wouldn't be renewed.

The chair told me that the entomologist was the one who'd discovered the fungus that dampened and altered the song of the *Q. tristeza* and which fungus, if the insect survived long enough, triggered an additional growth stage after the pupal stage, making the cicada, at adulthood, considerably larger than even its close North and Central American cousins and that also made its *exuvium* or moulting much tougher, and, with those discoveries, the entomologist had, in his own view if not that of his peers, made a contribution to the study of both the insect and the fungus. But then there was also the matter of his protocols; it was said that his *protocols*, above all, were sloppy—this, at least, was the best defense his colleagues here at the university had come up with, though they refused to characterize it as a *defense* and maintained, with absolute conviction, that they weren't trying to defend his reckless behavior, his truly monstrous behavior, first bringing *Q. tristeza* into the country without permission and without taking the proper steps to ensure it wouldn't be able to escape the laboratories at the university—no, serious academics would never defend such *sloppy* work, but they had an obligation to nevertheless attempt to understand and then characterize it for the so-called *lay* or *nonscientific community*, the chair said she'd been told; yes, she said, to characterize such work above all, so that others could understand its importance, even though the inevitable result of a set of *horribly sloppy* protocols was and could only have been a disaster, an actual disaster, still, this failure to follow normal protocols was not itself a malicious act (certainly *not* malicious, just *sloppy*; really, it had been the scientific laboratory's equivalent of a dropped and shattered dish, a mistake that was easy to make but difficult to clean up). No one, really no one, the chair stressed, not even among his peers in the academic community, would ever claim that his desperation—after all, the research summarized in the article he'd sent was, according to what those in his department said, potentially truly monumental, represented a major find, and this deserved to be widely reported, no matter its source; how many psychotropic insects were there, anyway? (the answer was, apparently, that there were so few as to make the journal's editors suspect the findings were totally fabricated)—was an excuse for his *mental break*, certainly not, his colleagues always added, how could it be? How many of them had had their own monumental findings dismissed—and here the chair couldn't resist mentioning her own work on what she insisted on referring to as *the discourse of Lyme disease*, papers, she said, languishing on some overworked editor's desk somewhere—just as unceremoniously and with as little justification?

But at the time, before anyone knew much about the entomologist's findings, everyone was simply horrified that this thing had happened on *our* campus, and that it wasn't a resident of the area who was responsible, as was the case up the coast in New Orleans, that it hadn't been a student either, as had happened in West Virginia, New York, Colorado, Kansas, Arkansas, Texas, Alabama, California, Delaware, New Jersey, Arizona, Nevada, Nebraska, Alaska, Oregon, Washington, Hawaii, Montana, Iowa, Indiana, and so on—no, this was one of the faculty. This was what shocked the chair the most, she told me: *How could it have been one of us?* she asked. A student, sure, or, more likely, a former student—we all, she told me, worried that some disturbed young man might take a comment the wrong way, or might feel (completely without reason, it went without saying, the chair said) that he'd gotten a grade much lower than the one he'd deserved; we all knew such students, the chair reminded me. This student, having taken his vengeance on the offending faculty member, or, and this, to the chair, was worse to contemplate, having found that faculty member not on campus that day, would proceed to start randomly firing at people in dumb retribution, whether from the top floor of the library or just out on the pseudo-quad. (It sounded, to me, as though she'd thought about this theoretical shooting in detail, and this idea was, I remember, fascinating to me.) But that it could be a faculty member? That was unthinkable, truly unthinkable to the chair. I didn't tell her about the puzzling panel meeting I'd had with the entomologist. I didn't tell her what the entomologist had said at that meeting. It felt too much like trying to grab the spotlight, too much like I would be trying to insert myself into the drama when really I had had no part in it, and I myself could only think about the people who'd been shot, the students and workers who'd died, and I didn't ever mention my only interactions with the entomologist, didn't mention the bird-thing on the roof (apparently, the subject of his study, a cicada, I now knew), didn't even think about the strange bird-thing until the chair told me about the entomologist's research.

Meanwhile, on the day of the shooting, the faculty member waiting with me in the Dean of Students's waiting room just stood and stared out the window, and I only barely understood what we were witnessing, and I found myself wandering to the doors again and again, as though to leave, and the faculty member with me, I remember, kept telling me to get away from the doors, to wait for *the all-clear*, and, at some point, I realized the student who'd been sitting behind the desk wasn't there anymore, and when we knocked on the doors leading down the hall to the dean's office, we didn't get any answer, and it took us some time to realize that all of the doors in the building were locked, and that *this* was the protocol we were supposed to be following in an *active shooter situation*. Altogether, we were there waiting for some signal that we could leave for almost four hours, and it was an hour and a half *after* a sheriff's deputy loudly announced who he was and told us we could leave that I even bothered to look at my phone to see that my wife had been calling and texting.

In Which

He Explains Some Arrangements, Tried at the Time

The dog, my feeling of doom in the Macy's, the broken bowl, the remnant in the garage, the classroom incident, the shooting—one of the things I've come to most distrust about language is that it makes things that can be communicated with even the tiniest bit of specificity seem as though they're being recalled perfectly in every detail, when, if I search my memory for any of these events, and even after all I've already said about them, I always discover that I in fact remember very little about their actual circumstances. When I try to remember the days that surround, for instance, the shooting, language covers over large gaps between events, thoughts, and sensations, and I would worry—worry *now*, I mean—that my memory was going, would worry, that is to say, if I'd ever had a particularly good memory. (And this was something—my average-to-poor memory—that my wife used against me often, demanding specifics from me when we argued about anything, precisely, I thought, because she knew I would never be able to recall what her exact words had been; for example, during the car ride home from a campus event celebrating the retirement of the department's longest-serving faculty member, a man accused of multiple instances of sexual harassment, when she'd made me so upset about our son's things. She, naturally, had a perfect command of specific details, even though her memory was neither better nor worse than mine or really anyone else's; instead, it seemed as though somehow her long-term memory worked best in moments of high stress and tension, at precisely the moments, I mean, that my own long-term memory seemed to fold.) When I'd tried to recall the meeting at which the chair had told us about the new active shooter protocol, I was temporarily distracted by my inability to remember whether it had also been the meeting at which the department's longest-serving faculty member argued that we didn't need a new sexual harassment policy because we already had one and had had no reported incidents the previous year (in part, another colleague said, *because* the present sexual harassment policy didn't require many such incidents be reported at all).

I could easily find out what day classes had started in the fall, and, by doing so, what date this meeting had been held, and I could then find the minutes from that Friday-before-the-first-day-of-classes meeting somewhere in my spam folder and see in the attachment to that email the item *New Active Shooter Protocol* and the list of people present, but the minutes would have nothing to tell me about the protocol itself, and they wouldn't touch on why I might have been distracted that day, what I'd thought about on the drive to campus, who I'd spoken to before the meeting, what I'd had for or even whether I'd eaten lunch that day, whether I had two cups of coffee or three, whether my wife and I had argued that morning, and so on, and because these were the things that, in my daily life, actually occupied most of my time and attention, the things that, when they were happening, seemed to me to *constitute* my life, I felt as though I'd forgotten most of what had happened and was left only with these few meaningless details. And outside of these meaningless details, my life then was even more inscrutable. I knew or thought I could remember that I went to school and taught my classes, and I'm certain I would know if I hadn't—our chair would, I'm sure, have found some way of replacing me that much sooner if I hadn't, even though doing so in the middle of the semester and at that particular time would have looked especially heartless, still, in relatively short order, I knew she would have been forgiven by my colleagues; she had tenure and was the chair (no one else wanted to be), so what were they going to do?—but I also thought I hadn't spent much time at the house then, and I couldn't think of where else I would have gone. I didn't drink. I didn't golf or go to the gym. I didn't *throw myself into my work.*

I do clearly remember the argument my wife and I had over what to do with our son's things, though. My wife wanted them gone because, she said, she didn't want to keep coming upon them the way we both did, on our way to the bathroom, in the middle of the night, with the streetlamp shining in through the first-closet-then-bedroom-and-now-closet-again window, or during the day, stopping us at the door for a moment when we wondered whether we ought to go in and straighten up and then decided not to, but I thought she would eventually be sorry if we gave it all away and there was nothing in the house left to remember him by (though now I can see this was really about my own feelings and not about hers, since, shamefully, her feelings weren't feelings I thought much about at that time), aside from the pictures in frames and on our phones. She told me if that was my feeling, I should take the things I wanted to keep and put them in the garage or else up in the attic because she couldn't keep walking past his room and breaking down, and that—me moving some of his things into the garage and giving away the rest—was our compromise, and I can remember thinking somewhere in all of that and despite myself (because I knew how wrong it was to be thinking it), how much what we were giving away had cost us, and how we might wish we'd kept some of it someday.

(And there was something pathetic in the things I gathered together in the garage, because, I thought, they'd been removed from their proper context. At first, I didn't know what to do with them and worried I was in some way dishonoring them by leaving them in the small U-Haul box on the rough wooden shelf in the garage, and I'm sure it was this worry that, in part, pushed me to the remaking, as I then mistakenly saw it, of my son.)

And while I can't remember that beginning of the semester meeting, I can remember the announcements of *workshops* on campus dealing with the *campus community's trauma* that fall, after the triple suicide in North Hall, the student-athlete dorm, led

by professionals the administration had been pressured into hiring
by the repeated occurrence of somewhat controversial and entirely
ad hoc *workshops* (which were really, it seemed to me, cable-TV-
versions of group therapy, guided by the remarks—in emails everyone received—from professors in the social sciences who might
once have produced papers on studies done of such things but
had never, themselves, led one and who prefaced their remarks
by saying they were not and had never been *practicing*, but were
simply academics with some knowledge of best practices and the
way these kinds of things generally went) conducted instead of
holding class, by faculty members with absolutely no background
in such things; I can also remember how much talk there'd been
before department meetings that semester about what students
had said in these sessions and how heartbreaking it was (we were
of course cautioned, repeatedly, by the administration, never to say
that what was said was outlandish or overblown, always to *honor*
students and their feelings), and also the reports about the some-
times-disturbing things students said during these sessions (suicidal
thoughts, we were reminded, should be reported immediately). I
can remember, I mean, that there *were* such workshops, though I
didn't attend any of them—my wife of course said *of course* I had
refused to attend them, *of course* I had, all said bitterly—in part because of the way these workshops were advertised and the fact that
I knew they would only partly be led by professionals, only partly,
but mostly really led by representatives of the administration, as
was almost always the case with things like these workshops; the
professionals would do the actual work of the workshop, calmly
and patiently listening to what each person said, not challenging
what was said but helping others in the room to *find their voices*,
but all of this would be prefaced by someone from HR telling,
once again, the story of how their cousin had killed himself years
ago after returning home from Afghanistan and how they'd felt
guilt in the immediate aftermath simply because they'd been there
and hadn't done anything to prevent it, and even though it wasn't
them who'd fired the shot that killed their cousin, still, we had to

understand that they could relate to what the workshop's participants—who were, the HR person would add, all here voluntarily (even though we'd of course all been informed that participation in these workshops would be monitored, and a refusal to *engage* could mean higher costs of liability in the future, and so we were *encouraged* to attend one of these workshops as soon as our schedules allowed (and in particular, research funding was explicitly tied to this *encouragement*, as the chair told us during the department meeting, which didn't affect me, as I'd been rendered ineligible for such funding through a decision made the previous semester by the college's dean, a decision that in turn meant, now, that there was no incentive whatsoever for me to attend one of these workshops, even though I was one of the only members of the department who'd been recently *personally affected by loss*, and so one of the only members of the department everyone could agree would benefit from the experience)), and so, because we'd all agreed that there was a problem, we'd actually already begun to solve that problem (the professional hired to lead the workshop would, I sincerely hoped, make some sort of face as though involuntarily during this ridiculous, self-serving monologue)—what *the administration* (and here there would be, I knew, a pause), *the administration, students, and faculty, all of us, the* whole *campus community*, were going through at this *very difficult time*.

My wife, I thought, thought that I avoided these kinds of things purely because I believed I could resolve my problems myself, and out of some stubbornness or recalcitrance she had, I thought, once, long ago, in fact *admired* as determination and perseverance, but which she now detested because its persistence meant I simply couldn't be moved on certain things, and this made me difficult to deal with both in the near term, when I stubbornly refused to hear other ideas and opinions, and also, unfortunately, in the long term, when, after some time, I would finally come around to her way of thinking and even loudly and repeatedly regret my earlier stubbornness and, she said *beat myself up over nothing*. Really, though, at the time, I had a certain amount of respect for the work the professionals seemed to be doing with the students, and even some curiosity about the workshops themselves, but then I was put off by the commonplaces my colleagues returned with from these workshops and my own experiences with the group our social worker had recommended my wife and I attend (and which group I had, after the second meeting, told my wife conflicted with a committee schedule, and so, afterwards, only she attended these group meetings, and, after a few weeks of going by herself, she stopped bothering to tell me what had happened and how much she thought it was helping, and started staying longer at these meetings, and I can remember wanting to start going again then but feeling as though doing so would show the bad faith that had led to my not going in the first place and then I remember I just felt trapped inside the decision I'd made), and I couldn't be sure whether these commonplaces were the products of my colleagues' own thinking or were the actual language used in the workshops, and so I held firm in my decision not to attend.

In Which
He Tells a Story

Overnight after our visit to the Macy's, in my mind (I didn't sleep well, and I felt it would be better to focus on something else), and then in the morning in my notes, I made some last-minute changes to the story-lecture I'd planned to deliver the day of the shooting and with which I was now, through the pure chance of the catty-corner neighbor's suicide and my cancelled classes, instead going to conclude the course. I'd first conceived of this particular story-lecture in response, I think, to complaints after the story-lecture on the shem, Rabbi Loew, and the Golem of Prague, complaints from a group of the better students (who, I heard saying to each other, had been warned about me and my classes, but who had, at first, after my story-lecture on Adam and the naming of the animals, felt reassured that they still might get something out of the course, but who were now either confused or disappointed and thinking about withdrawing after all), and I intended to focus on what happened after the fall of the Tower of Babel, after the ur-Akkadian language had been split into its dialects—this, I thought, couldn't fail but to seem perfectly appropriate for and even expected by the class—but then something during the semester or else many somethings during the semester had changed my idea of the story I would be telling, or maybe those things just convinced me that what I intended to focus on wasn't something worth focusing on after all; the events of that week undoubtedly played their part in the change in focus, too.

Of course by this point in the week, classes and final exams had been cancelled altogether, though I didn't know this the morning of the final day of classes—no one had called to tell me and I hadn't checked my school email (and wouldn't have checked the university's social media under any circumstances; there was, anyway, the power outage at home, and then the trip to the Macy's; later, I would think how strange it was that the university routinely sent out text messages cancelling classes for hurricanes and tornadoes but hadn't done so for this, and maybe, I thought, this was the result of yet more bad legal advice, or of ignoring wiser legal advice). Interruptions and sudden cancellations had long ago ceased to be extraordinary, and so, when I pulled into a nearly empty parking lot, I didn't think much about it. Everyone's schedule had been corrupted that semester—classes met, when they met, at the campus student center, or in instructors' offices, assignments and even midterms were called off without advance notice, and the administration kept changing its so-called *educational and curricular priorities* (there were rumors the Board of Regents would soon have to step in)—so there was little expectation from students or other observers that instructors would follow the plans laid out in their syllabi at the beginning of the term. For the most part, the only students still attending were those who were determined to pressure their instructors into returning to business-as-usual as soon as possible (these students emailed me constantly, asking about their grades and demanding to know whether a cancelled class or the pushing back of an assignment's deadline would affect the release of their transcripts; also, they were confused about how the words of the angel to Abraham at the binding of Isaac were relevant to this course and was there any way to make up the extra credit they'd missed?) and those whose continued attendance was, very simply, a complete surprise to me. The latter group of students were students who'd shown up only sporadically, if ever, earlier in the term (some I didn't recognize at all and I had to check the tiny pictures on the roster I'd printed out at the beginning of the term to be sure these were, actually, my students), and so when I later learned that I'd held this class that shouldn't have been held, I wondered whether, like me, they maybe hadn't checked their email the day before, or whether somehow they'd failed to learn about the shooting—these were, after all, students who'd missed weeks of class at a time and at least one of whom had, for instance, sent me emails on both Founders' Day and again on MLK Day asking, passive-aggressively, whether she'd missed the email I'd sent telling students that class had been cancelled. (Maybe, this student suggested, I should use a different messaging app?) These students, I knew, wouldn't mind that the lecture they were hearing bore no resemblance to other classes—most of them wouldn't notice the difference anyway—and the other students, the strivers, would complain no matter what happened in class and would ask endlessly for simple and clear answers to their confused questions, and so, at least to start with that morning, I felt free to simply tell the story in the way I'd chosen, though it bore very little resemblance to the story I'd wanted to tell when I'd first conceived of it.

This story began long before the tower was finished, I told the nearly empty auditorium, before anyone even thought it could be finished. There was, at that time, a young man in Eriku named Banda, a tradesman who could find no work and who spent his days idly. His father and his father's father, and his father's father's father before him had all built their own homes, each generation building a bigger and more opulent home, first in clay, then in stone, then in stone with gold ornaments, all according to the constellation above by which the city had been laid out, but Banda, born with eleven fingers and under an unlucky star, couldn't put food on the table with his work, and he'd lost hope of buying a plot for his own home. His father's business was still strong; because people knew his father, and knew his father's work, they chose his father over many other builders in the city, including Banda, who was only able to maintain a semblance of pride because his father sometimes offered him jobs he couldn't himself take on. Neither his father nor his mother would allow his wife to live under their roof, however, and, because she'd given birth in the spring, and because her parents threatened to take the child and raise him as their own, Banda's inability to make a living weighed very heavily on him.

Banda was not alone in his predicament—young men like him went without work all over the city. These young men, after, in the mornings, trying and failing to find paying work, spent their days wandering from one tavern to another; when the tavern's keeper noticed them lingering too long over their beer, or when their credit had worn itself thin, they would be shooed out into the street, and would, on their empty stomachs and dazed by the sun and beer, stagger from one tavern to the next, looking for a friend whose table they could join so that they could postpone the moment when they had to return to their family homes, where only their sisters' withering gazes and their wives' pity awaited them, and where, they knew, they would once again have their wounds of pride reopened and their failures exposed. Given the state of things, Eriku being what it was, it was inevitable that these young men would see each other often in the taverns, and that they would come to recognize the similarity of their predicaments, and that they would then begin talking to one another.

In fact this happened frequently, and often enough in the same dusty tavern near the same nearly empty bazaar across an expanse of untilled land outside of the city's walls. The young men preferred this tavern because it had no other customers and so its proprietor only shooed them away when she wanted a nap, or when she had some other business (she was, Banda heard rumored, besides a tavern keeper and a prostitute, also a small-time moneylender, and it was the last two aspects of the business that made money and allowed her to keep the tavern open). Her beer was so weak that it seemed to have been first brewed before Banda's father's father's father's time, but this didn't matter to the young men, as they were only there to escape the blinding sun and the reproaches of their families, and, besides, the tavern keeper was talkative and friendly and gave credit freely.

When Banda and his friends asked the tavern keeper why she kept this tavern in this place, this crumbling place not even within the city walls of Eriku, this out-of-the-way bazaar where there were no people, when, with only a little more money (and, although they didn't say it, with a better brew), she could certainly move to a more prosperous area in Eriku, the tavern keeper told them that the tavern had been her mother's, and her mother's mother's before her, and what else could she do? She had to make a living somehow.

This city, the tavern keeper told them, or this bazaar and the buildings that surrounded it, had been intended to become a great city and had, long before, been the seat of power of a king, one who ruled over Eriku, too, but whose fate, it was said, was to build an even greater city. This city was now, it was true, disused and avoided, and this was because—and this Banda and his friends might not know, the tavern keeper told them I told my students—of the bad end the former king had come to: He'd been hanged and dragged behind a chariot around Eriku's walls until his limbs separated from his body, and many of the courtiers who had inhabited this new city with him had met the same fate, so that, for a time, it was said that no one at all lived in the new city, and the only people who traveled there were Eriku's bandits and rogues, who, seeing that the place had been abandoned, had taken up residence there. Even though, the tavern keeper told Banda and his friends, this was really just a rumor and only partly true (some courtiers and retainers had survived and, because they knew they weren't welcome in Eriku, remained in the abandoned city, and couldn't show their faces in Eriku for fear of retribution), the malicious reputation of the abandoned city had nonetheless spread, and the citizens of Eriku avoided even speaking of the existence of this city.

After his death, the tavern keeper told Banda and his friends, it came out that the king had sold off many of Eriku's treasures in his efforts to build his new city, and, in particular, in order to buy the materials with which to build its ziggurat, the Temple of the Seven Lights of the Earth, a temple that, it was said, no priest had ever asked for and that would have had no worshipers had it ever been finished, as it was widely known that this king was godless and cruel and the structure he proposed was said to be blasphemous, intended not just to rival the heavens in height but in fact to climb higher; the king had ruled through fear, and his grisly fate was only a faint echo, as it were, of what he'd done to his enemies when he'd been alive, and worshiping in a temple built by such a man was, it was said, unthinkable.

The story went that this king had had a son, a beautiful prince everyone had loved and whose smile was said to shine like the breaking of dawn on the river, a boy who was as wise and as courageous as he was beautiful, and who, it was said, the king had come to envy for the affections—his wives', his concubines'—this king felt the boy had stolen from him. The king punished him for the slightest offense and kept him locked up in the palace from one sunset to the next, but the boy remained happy and still all who saw him couldn't imagine a better-tempered boy. No matter how harshly the king punished his son, the tavern keeper told Banda and his friends, the prince's good nature always showed through, and he always forgave his father, saying, *He does what he does, and I do what I do*, and this magnanimity aroused yet more sympathy from the wives, concubines, and courtiers, and this sympathy in turn made the king more resentful toward his son.

One day, the son of a stable hand, a young man who, though he was in fact several years older than the king's son, looked very young, nearly the same age as the prince, and who'd often played with the prince through the windows of the palace, decided to rescue the boy by hiding him in one of his own father's wagons, one he'd made to look like one of the palace's wagons, smuggling him out of the palace and then off to his father's home in Eriku. Unfortunately, the king was a suspicious ruler, and stopped the strange wagon himself before it could pass out of the palace gates. *I only know what I know about what happened next because my mother's father worked as stable master to the king*, the tavern keeper told Banda and his friends, I told the students. *I was always told that the prince, who had been clothed and made up to look like the stable hand's son, was pulled down off the wagon by the king and was then crushed when the ass pulling the wagon startled and ran off with the wagon. Because of this disguise, it took many days before the stable hand's son could be found and the identity of the boy who'd been mangled at the palace could be known with any certainty, and the neglect and disrespect with which the boy's body had been treated when it was thought to be the stable hand's son's—but which body, it was then found, had in fact been the prince's—then made the king furious. He ordered that those who'd disposed of the body be executed, and this had, in a roundabout way, precipitated the violent rebellion that followed, because,* the tavern keeper told Banda and his friends, *it turned the citizens more fully against him.*

The temple the king then began building, everyone seemed to agree, the tavern keeper told Banda and his friends, was a monument not to Marduk, as the king said he intended, but instead to the king's self-pity, an obvious attempt to obscure his own evil conduct from posterity. Because the son crushed by the wagon had been this king's only child, and because the king himself had been executed by his subjects, the temple, still unfinished three generations later, was the only sign left of this infamous chapter in Eriku's history, and all of Eriku's subsequent kings had left it and the surrounding city unfinished and untouched because it would only incur yet more expense to tear them down. How appreciative would their current king be if Banda and his friends—who, the tavern keeper pointed out, had all the necessary expertise—tore it down and relegated the whole sad history to legend? Perhaps then, the tavern keeper said, I told my students, more work would come to Banda and his friends, well-paying work, too, from the king and his family.

But, the tavern keeper said, there was another possibility, I told my students: Banda and his friends could, instead, prove their worth by *finishing* the tower and the surrounding city, if they wished. Finished, the tower would be the tallest structure in sight, and pilgrims would come from far and wide to this city with the tower they could see from the hills that surrounded the valley in which Eriku lay. So that even if there were still some superstitious citizens who would spit at Banda and his friends for finishing the cursed tower—a tower, the tavern keeper said, that had been raised in an excess of pride, and that, she repeated in her strange, deep voice, was supposed to rival the height of the heavens (and for which reasons, it was said, the gods themselves had ensured its founder had come to such a bad end)—there would be many more people arriving in the new city, all of whom would need shelter, and who would therefore need someone to help build that shelter, and through this, Banda and his friends could finally make their fortunes.

And so, I told my students, Banda and his friends had two very different choices before them, but they didn't know that this tavern keeper was not at all what she seemed, for she wasn't a moneylender (though it was true that her family had lived in the quarter for generations, and it was also true that she was a prostitute of a sort), and she kept the stall open with money she'd inherited, for her mother's father wasn't, after all, the stable master at the infamous king's palace and this was the moment that two campus police officers entered the classroom, and, after *securing the building* and reporting that fact into their very loud radios (I'd heard them before the officers even entered the auditorium, and briefly panicked that yet another shooting was taking place outside), told us that the campus was closed and all classes had been cancelled, and asked us all to please *disperse in an orderly fashion.*

In Which
He Visits the Police, Again

I've always wondered whether the administration had been some-how forced to turn the matter of the student who'd thrown acid in the other student's face over to the police after the shooting brought their attention to campus—even though of course the two things were completely unrelated—or whether the administration, in its never-ending effort to avoid as many civil suits as possible, had simply given up on trying to keep the matter in-house and finally turned it over to the proper authorities, or if it was just a simple matter of the victim's family forcing the university's hand. In any case, I was, once again, called upon to give a statement at the police station, and, this being a small town, that also meant dealing with several of the same officers I'd already dealt with. In a different time, this might have made me seem suspicious and even worthy of investigation, but these officers were so overworked I'm not sure they even noticed I was there in front of them for the fourth time in less than a year. I later learned that the boy, the acid thrower, had told some story about having headaches and not being able to sleep because of the noise many students staying in the dorms complained about and that was thought, at the time, to have been a faulty transformer but all of the transformers near the dorms were discovered to have been operating normally, and this might have led only to expulsion and the recommendation of mental health treatment if the crime hadn't been so horrible and if it hadn't ultimately been reported to the police, but, as I've said, he'd already left the country by the time the police were called in so all of those thoughts were moot.

Though I can no longer remember the exact date or when precisely, in relation to the last day of classes or the day I turned in grades, this was, I do remember that it was around this time—the same week I gave my statement to the police, I think—that I hit the man walking his bicycle on campus. Because it was summer and grading, such as it was, had been largely a matter of simply totaling up the few grades the students had earned much earlier in the semester and being slightly more generous than I would normally have been in rounding, I had very little to do, and because campus had been completely closed for a week or so, I at first spent more time at home, but my wife was still also often staying home, calling in sick to work, as she'd done seemingly all spring, and it became clear very quickly that, because she knew I liked quiet, my presence in the house wouldn't help her to feel better—in fact, she told me directly, me being there made her more stressed—and so I understood after the first week of this that I'd have to find some other place to be during the days, and the sooner I established that routine, the better for both of us.

My routine was, in the end, simple: I drove to campus, went to my office, and read the newspaper on my laptop until I couldn't stand to be in my office anymore, then I got up and walked around the floor my office was on until I thought I saw someone else or found evidence that someone else was there, on campus, in their office, and then I took the elevator down to the ground floor and walked first to the student union, then around it to the office of the registrar and the human resources wing of the administrative building (avoiding the pseudo-quad and the grassy area behind the library, where there were still signs of the investigation laid out in places and also, occasionally, people—not typically police—examining them), then back to my own building, by which time I'd be sweating profusely and would stop at the water fountain to fill my mug before going back up in the elevator to my office, to wait for lunch, after which I could run an errand or two and return home around three in the afternoon, late enough that my wife would already be in bed or out running errands and I could sit at the table in the kitchen and do more nothing. After only about a week of this, though, people started to show up on campus, not students, faculty, or administrators, not, in other words, people who had any connection to the university whatsoever, but instead older people carrying signs that read things like *Ban IDIOTS Not GUNS* or *I have the RIGHT to defend Students* or *We Will Not Be DISARMED*, first just one or two of these people, clearly lost and confused in overalls and camouflage, wandering around until they found the yellow tape near the library, then whole crowds of them (though never more than ten or twelve at a time, and usually the same people—I could typically recognize them by their facial hair or their signs), chanting and ruining my pre-lunch walks.

While leaving campus one day, after one of these people, a man wearing jeans and a camouflage T-shirt with a Gadsden flag on the back, spat at me for reasons I couldn't understand, I hit a man walking his bicycle on the side of the road hard enough to dent the hood of the car and crack the windshield. I was, I remember, just turning out of the parking lot and still thinking about this man who'd spat at me and his inexplicable-to-me hatred or disgust; the turn was almost a blind turn because of the way the road curved out of sight immediately on the left, and so I was trying to look to see if there was any traffic coming from that direction and not, I guess, paying attention to the man walking in the gutter with his bike to the right of me. (Even though it was on campus, this wasn't a place that people apart from me ever walked, being next to the softball field parking lot, across a wide service road from the rest of the campus and basically totally isolated from any other campus facility, in a part of the campus without buildings or sidewalks—it was, nonetheless, the only place I could reliably find a parking space, and, even though it was now summer break, and perhaps only out of habit, I usually didn't bother to look for a spot closer to my office.) This man had almost no hair apart from the stubble on his face; he wore dirty jeans and an unbuttoned shirt, and he was walking his bicycle because, I thought later, he'd balanced a small rolling suitcase and a shopping basket—one of those handheld baskets (not a cart, in other words), filled with empties from the recycling bins on campus, I guessed; the end of the semester, I remember thinking, would have been an especially good time to round up empties, though I couldn't recall ever seeing people collecting them at that time (and this probably shouldn't have been a surprise, since this was a time I normally didn't go to campus in order to avoid seeing students who would only weep or complain about their grades)—on the bicycle's seat and rack and was holding a trash bag in his other hand, and this would later make me wonder how I could possibly have missed seeing him, but I did.

I didn't see him while turning, so I only knew I'd hit him because he and his trash bag were suddenly there, on the car's hood, this huge dark shape covering most of the windshield that made me stomp on the brakes, which then sent him jerking forward off the car and the bag flying, and I was so terrified that I didn't even think to put the car into park, so that when I opened the door and took my foot off the brake pedal to step out and the car lurched forward, I had to awkwardly slide back in and stomp on the brake again to put the car in park, and this—the surprise of it—made me shake and cry, and for a moment I didn't realize I'd pulled something, a muscle, very painful, in my groin because of the way I'd gotten out of the car and gotten back into it. Fortunately, the man was lying on the asphalt about another foot in front of the car, so I didn't run him over, but I remember being extremely shaky and unable to control myself, and I remember he was somehow calm and still coherent enough to help himself up and try to bend over to check on the bicycle now next to the car in the grass on the side of the road. Empties were rolling around the road in front of us, and, as soon as he'd seen the bike was intact and even though the back wheel was now slightly bent, he started collecting his empties—very, very slowly—and I followed him around, limping and weeping and trying to get ahead of him to pick up a can or a bottle before he bent over to do so and also just trying to get his attention, but too clumsy from my muscle pull and crying and adrenaline to offer any real help. He smelled awful,

I remember, and he was slick with sweat—it was a hot day, and it was so humid my hair was wet just from the walk to the car—but even so I wanted to reach out and hold him, to still him, and so, when he got close enough, I grabbed him by both shoulders and brought him close, shushing him and trying to pat his back while he pushed back against me somewhat weakly. He seemed particularly sensitive about his left shoulder. Though there was a scrape on his left elbow that was bleeding—some of the blood, I saw later, had gotten on my shirt—and some obvious road rash on his back to which the back of his shirt was sticking (there was also some sort of stain on his pants, though I remember thinking that it looked like it had set long ago and so couldn't be related to the accident), he seemed ready to go on about his business with no help from me.

For what seemed like forever but was probably more like four or five minutes, I tried to get the man's attention so that I could get him into the car and drive him to the hospital, but, after his violent reaction to my attempted embrace, I was reluctant to touch him again, and he wouldn't meet my eyes no matter how I approached him. I pulled out my phone and started looking through my contacts for campus security, but, while I scrolled through the list, not really seeing the individual entries, reading them again and again and finally realizing I didn't have the number in my phone and then realizing I didn't have service here anyway, the man had meanwhile collected enough of his loose empties that he'd started off again down the road, holding the bike up just slightly at the back to help the bent wheel. I wasn't exactly sure, I remember, what I would tell campus security if I got a signal and could get them on the phone—*I hit someone, but he doesn't want to talk to me and I'm sorry I'm crying, I'm trying to stop. Can you help me, please?*— so I got in the car and drove slowly forward to catch up to the man, then I switched lanes and pulled alongside him, telling him to please get in, I'd take him to the hospital, he wouldn't have to pay for anything. Instead, though, he turned off the road and into the grass, which seemed to make pushing the bike harder—he was struggling to move it forward at the same pace he was walking and he was walking very slow—but it was clear he didn't want anything to do with me, so I pulled over to the curb and sat in the car for at least ten minutes, watching him disappear into the woods and then just sat there, crying, until I finally felt calm enough to leave. I remember I turned the key in the ignition, thinking the car was off, and the horrible noise the car made, and I remember driving so slowly and looking in every direction, and I remember slamming on the brakes so many times on the trip home, at the light bouncing suddenly into my peripheral vision from the reflection of the sun on someone else's side mirror, at a dog playing by itself in a fenced yard set back from the road, at other cars stopped at red lights, and I remember I drove very slowly even on the highway with cars piling up behind me and then passing me, slowly enough that I eventually pulled over altogether and sat in the car without moving for some time, thinking I'd walk the rest of the way home even though I was in pain, or else I'd call a taxi, but then I knew I'd still need to come out to pick up the car and drive it home at some point—my wife never would—and I remember I'd wanted to just get it over with, to get the car home and then never drive it again.

And after that, until we both moved out and even long after, I didn't drive at all. My wife drove us everywhere when she was home and we needed something, and if she was at work, I either didn't do anything that I would have to drive to or else I walked. This situation was difficult—the town was relatively small population-wise but it was also very spread out, and it was always hot and humid outside, so much so that the news routinely warned *older citizens* to stay indoors, drink plenty of fluids, and avoid heatstroke—and not driving meant that when my wife was home, I was also, typically, home. If I spent those days in our bedroom, as I tried to do at first, my wife told me she felt I was purposefully excluding her from something, but after a few tense days, I found that, when I was in the garage, she didn't say anything about me not being around; maybe the thought of me sweating and swatting away mosquitoes made her feel I was punishing myself just enough that she didn't need to pile on or add to my problems.

After I'd completely cleaned out the garage, and after I'd found the old fan in the laundry room, it wasn't awful to just sit there as long as I wasn't moving around too much—I mean that I didn't sweat so much and the mosquitoes couldn't land on me if I was sitting directly in front of the fan—but I still had nothing to do, or anyway nothing I wanted to do, and I began to notice similarities to my son's room in the shape and dimensions of the space, and so I arranged things so that it would look more like his room. I really think I did this simply out of sitting there so many hours, in front of the fan, hour after hour, sweat tickling me just at my hairline, thinking about the things I could have been doing and trying not to think about the things I could have been doing and staring at the box of his things on the worktable in the garage and trying to think of stories I could tell in the unlikely event I found a new teaching job.

On

His Work in the Garage,
a Brief Explanation

I can't account for the thing I spent so much time on also being the thing I most wanted to keep hidden from other people other than to say that this seems—to me—like the normal state of things (though I don't know whether it really is some general state everyone inhabits or if it's yet another thing that frustrates my wife and colleagues, some of whom (many? all?) seem to have no problem whatsoever talking about the things they're working on and in fact talk endlessly about projects they've completed, even years after completing them). I guess I wouldn't be asking the question if I didn't suspect that this was, in fact, at least somewhat out of the ordinary, but I also feel there must be something in everyone's life that occupies a great deal of their time and yet is also a thing they're not only not proud of but that they would go to any length to keep hidden, and I wonder if the real difference is that this thing, for me, in that time, was an actual physical thing, something tangible, rather than a set of worries or anxieties or fears (the things, in other words, that I think others spend so much time on but that they rarely, if ever, reveal).

(My wife, during our time together, has complained about this habit or trait of mine, of course, but she has also complained about many or even most aspects of my personality at some point or another—about, for instance, my deep hatred of consciously repeating myself, though she is of course aware that I frequently do repeat myself and that what I hate is, in fact, being *asked* to repeat myself, since I believe (and, really, can I be wrong to believe this? I can't completely convince myself that I'm wrong) that when people ask me to repeat myself (usually, in fact, the one asking is my wife, so her skepticism is, I would say, not entirely pure), they're indicating a certain degree of inattention, and, through that inattention, also a lack of respect, first, for me, naturally, but then also for my ideas and the thoughts I've chosen to share; there's also this matter, more recent than my other failings though still not *so* recent, of having a tendency towards a certain level of opacity or even, frankly, confusion in my speech, which my wife complained about when we still spoke regularly—justly, I think—and that, I felt then, contributed to a certain unattractive *glee* she seemed to feel in pointing out the contradictions she saw (I often didn't see them) in what I said—when, I mean, she was even able to understand what I'd said, which was considerably less frequently than before the accident (though, in saying this, I don't mean to imply a deficit on her part; I fully acknowledge how confusing my speech could be, especially around the time of the accident), and which tendency then eventually made the telling of stories seem more and more attractive, since stories, I found, tended to focus and structure what I had to say in a way I couldn't manage otherwise, and then this eventually resulted both in the story-lectures I began to develop and in the way I tried to interact with my wife, who had little patience with it in fact. (My wife's glee at my confused speech, I should probably say, was often accompanied by or was later explained as a reaction to what seemed to me to be willful misunderstandings of what I'd said (or at least, what I'd tried to say), interpretations of the way in which my words or my tone might have been understood, for instance, by someone who had really no sympathy for me or my position and who was disinclined to give me or my words the benefit of any doubt whatsoever, which is to say, someone who just plain disliked me, and who wanted to see me fail, rather than someone—like, for instance, my wife, or what might be expected from such a person—who cared for me and who might even, to some limited degree, have depended upon me and my success, and so wished to see me succeed. I should

emphasize, though, because I've been misunderstood in exactly
this way before, that I'm *not* saying that what I said or how I said
it was in some way beyond her or else somehow over her head—I
worry that both my way of putting things and even the thought
itself might be construed as an insult to her intelligence when they
aren't; I was, often and even long before this period of more intense
confusion, only just working out my thoughts when I spoke, and
this was even more often the case when I spoke to my wife, since
that was a situation in which I'd always—probably foolishly—
counted on a sort of privilege, in that I could, with her as with few
others, be free to work things out while talking rather than thinking about them obsessively and then, after considerable thought,
come up with some pithy way of saying them (which would then
necessarily also be a way of saying them that lacked all nuance
or complexity) that, nonetheless, would be subject to a general
but low-level misunderstanding, speaking, then, with my wife in
a way that I'd always hoped would encourage her to respond in
kind and so engage in something more truly like what I'd always
wanted out of conversation and not, in other words, a *discussion*,
a word that meant, to me, because of my job, I guess, an exchange
of rhetoric (and therefore an attempt at manipulation on the part
of those involved), and, indeed, she did sometimes talk to me in
that way, in her most unguarded moments, adding concerns that
I hadn't yet thought about, or asking for clarification on some essential aspect of the thing that, once again, because I was speaking
extemporaneously, I hadn't yet fully considered, or to which I had
given very little consideration, and always in a tone of voice that
conveyed actual concern and care, and this tone of voice was distinct enough to put me at ease when I heard it, and its absence was
also then perfectly obvious and liable to change, in turn, my own
tone of voice and my way of thinking about my wife's reactions.
And then I'd also often practiced my lectures at home with my son
before I gave them to my students, having long before found that
the simple act of speaking my thoughts aloud offered me the best
opportunity to find what I would otherwise miss in what I was

trying to communicate (but also, and before we'd had our son, through recording what I was saying in the car and then playing it back to make lecture notes), that my very first such attempts were always nearly incomprehensible and exceedingly confusing, and, again, all this was long before the accident, and it became a habit I couldn't shake, even after my wife complained about my confused speech, even to the point of saying that I should probably seek help for it, that I was scaring her, and not making any sense, and our social worker, too, was concerned, and it was around that point that I decided that it would be better simply not to answer when asked questions, and to allow the silence that inevitably followed to go on and on unless and until I knew for certain what I was about to say would make some sort of acceptable sense to the person asking, and, even though I'd tried the speech-acts-language and the agglutinative English, it was only through the stories I told and retold that I began to feel really confident that my ideas were coming through, and then afterwards, those stories took on an added significance as a result.))

But let me make myself clear here by returning to specifics: The thing I'd wanted to keep hidden for as long as possible, the thing into which I poured hours and hours, was the recreation of my son's room, in the garage. It was, I should say, a process that had begun haphazardly and without purpose, but with very little else to occupy me, it quickly came to seem more and more important.

In fact it began the same afternoon I removed the remnant from the wall, though I didn't think of it in that way at the time. I remember I placed the egg on the worktable to get it up and out of the way, and, when it wobbled forward after I'd set it down and threatened to fall off the table, I steadied it with one of my son's toys. This, at least, is how I remember it beginning: simply, practically, like the barber's washbasin before Don Quixote repurposed it as a helmet; the only other object on the table at that time was the box of things I'd saved from my son's room. A week or so later, sitting in the lawn chair next to the fan and passing my eyes over some book whose title I can no longer recall, I remember I looked over at the egg and, in that moment, like the lights of a car pulling into a driveway playing on the ceiling inside, saw a very slight resemblance, because of the pegboard behind it, to a human torso, one of my son's approximate size, with the holes of the pegboard above it looking, from where I sat, not unlike mouth, eyes, and nose, and then the whole thing resolving once again into egg, pegboard, toy. The egg had been cracked where it was dented, and inside I thought, for the briefest of instants, I saw something move—a bug or, worse, a rodent—and I think I wouldn't have been able to bear to see such a thing, so I slipped one of my son's shirts on over the egg, purely, at the time, to cover up this crack, and then, as though I'd set out to do so all along, I stood the toy I'd used to steady the egg on the table on its head and stuck its feet into the shirt's armhole and, when it wouldn't stay like that, I pulled an old rubber band I found in the top drawer of the work-table up over the toy and around the cuff, to help keep the arm in place to steady the egg.

Elsewhere, I think, I've spoken about or at least mentioned Barry, the wrestler, the toy I'd used as an arm. Because most of the other things in the box were soft—stuffed animals, a blanket, some clothes—Barry was really the only thing in the box suited to the purpose, but in that moment, looking at the toy upside down in its sleeve, I remember thinking it would have been a good choice even if there had been other possibilities; Barry, I remember thinking, would have been my son's choice, too, though subsequently I've been made to realize this thought was, as it must seem to every-one else naturally, horribly depraved and even ghoulish. Now, as I've mentioned before, I'm much less certain I understood what my son—or anyone at all, especially those closest to me—actually wanted, or I guess now I feel more certain I am in fact mistaken about what he wanted (and of course it is, now, much too late to correct such mistakes), but at the time I remember I felt as though, by placing the toy, Barry, as I'd placed it, I'd begun to understand something that had been hidden from me for a long time.

On

Painting and Decoration

Months earlier, it would have been easy to do what it then occurred to me to do, so easy, in fact, I remember it caused a fleeting
sort of absolute despair in me; not only would it have been easy to
accomplish what I sought to accomplish if I'd only thought to do
it then, I thought, at the time, but if it had occurred to me to do
then what I'd decided to do now, I wondered if possibly things between my wife and I wouldn't have been quite so poisoned, which
is to say I felt almost certain they would *not* have been, though I
can also acknowledge, now, that her sense of betrayal could only
have been much worse, and so, really, all this would have accomplished would have been to delay her hurt rather than to heal it or
narrowly avoid creating or causing it. In any case, rather than argue
over what and how much I was trying to keep of our son's stuff,
rather than rashly accuse my wife of having thrown out something
I claimed meant so much to me only to find that thing later and
feel guilty about how I'd treated her and the way I'd felt about her
and her actions (which were revealed, then, to not have been her
actions at all), I could have simply pretended to go along with
all my wife was proposing to get rid of, could have even volun-
teered—I hope I wouldn't have been so debased that I claimed,
after volunteering, to be sparing her feelings in doing so, or even
to claim I was *doing it for her*, though I'm not sure I wouldn't have
said something along those lines if, later, she said I was, once again,
not listening to her, not thinking through what something meant
to her—to dispose of everything myself. I'd like to think I would
have had the good sense to take first a few boxes, smaller things,

put them in the trunk of the car, tell my wife I'd drop them off at Goodwill on my way to school, and then, later, when I could be sure she wouldn't see me, bring those boxes to the garage, and to then repeat this process for perhaps a week, giving her time to grieve but also preserving the plausibility that I was actually disposing of these things and not simply bringing them across the yard, to the garage, though I also feel sure I would have done it all in a single day, while she was at work, making my wife suspicious of me—*A band-aid*, I might have said, *I just had to rip it off like a band-aid*, though I don't think she would have thought this was at all plausible, knowing me as well as she did—and ultimately leading to arguments other than the ones we had, but arguments nonetheless.

As it was, though, I had only the one box of things I'd managed to negotiate keeping. Everything else had, actually, really been donated to Goodwill or else thrown away. In order to remake my son's room in the garage, then, I had to paint on the bare concrete the pattern of the tiny rug that he'd played on, and, when my clumsy painting with its warped corners and ragged edges didn't capture the effect, I painted around my painted rug the wood of the floors inside. I painted, on the walls of the garage, the high shelves and the animal-faced boxes that had sat on them. I painted the window opposite them, and, in it, its view of the neighbor's porch. I painted the dresser on the garage door. I put the few toys I'd rescued where I thought my son would have wanted them to go. I wept. I laid out his clothes, tried to find a place for his blanket that wouldn't expose the whole artifice quite so starkly. The trouble was that the place continued to feel hollow, empty, and, even though I'd agonized over the details, and all of this had taken a week, still, my painting was poor, and didn't even really fool the eye, and I knew, of course I knew, what it was it was missing.

On

His Son, the Materials of Which He Was Made

The egg didn't roll off the table with the wrestler in place, but still it wobbled, and I could see it would need another support to stay in place, so I chose the baseball glove, a gift from his grandmother; it wasn't broken in at all, and could stand up, stiff, without flopping over or folding. There was, I admit, a certain amount of laziness in the choice of the glove—as a glove, I thought, it naturally made sense as a kind of hand, even though it was also, in this context, completely out of proportion with the rest of the figure I'd begun to form, and left no room for an arm. I'd kept this glove because it was one of the few things my wife's mother had given our son, and I couldn't or I guess *didn't* believe my wife really wanted to get rid of it (though of course she *did* want to get rid of it, and wasn't, in general, a sentimental person, just one prone to sadness when confronted with such an awful situation, as anyone would be; she, in fact, wanted everything gone—who would use it? it could only hurt now). This glove was black with white lacing and an illegible white signature, and, being leather, was heavy, or would have been heavy (and no doubt also too large and cumbersome) for him had he ever shown any desire to put it on; as it was, he was too young even to understand what its purpose was, and the only time I could remember him playing with it was the time I'd walked in on him in his room on the floor, with Hugbee sitting on it, folded over. My wife's mother had always seemed frustrated with my wife and me after the birth of our son (maybe before it, too), frustrated, I mean, because when she asked what we needed, what he needed,

we always told her that the boy, really, had enough toys, enough
clothes, too many even, too many anyway, to keep track of (we
meant, as I think she understood, too many *for us*, too many toys
and clothes for either one of us to worry about the boy losing
and the inevitable scene that would follow when we couldn't find
them), and this had led to our claiming that, because he already
had so much, we didn't really know what *else* he wanted—maybe
nothing, at least right now—and so she'd been put in the position
of not spending much time with the boy (she lived far away, and
wasn't well enough to travel) and not getting useful information
from the people who *did* spend time with him, all of which resulted in the gifting of things my son hadn't wanted—not really, not
as demonstrated by the frequency with which he expressed any interest in those things—or at least things he didn't play with much
after they'd been given to him.

In fact, this process—this process, I mean, of our working
backward from some conclusion that really, ultimately, only reflected a personal laziness on our part (though it was also, often
if not always, a conclusion shared between the two of us (maybe
then, *personal* isn't quite the right word, though I think such conclusions could only have seemed, let's say, *unique to my wife and
myself* to others))—or failure to think, I mean *truly* think, about
the desires our son might have had but which were, as yet, un-
fulfilled (a process, besides, that my wife and I had never really
discussed; it was, instead, always only implied, always, I mean,
lurking below the surface of our every decision), working from
this point of refusing to accept our son as an agent in the world,
refusing, I mean, to think of our son as an actor, as, ultimately,
a fully fledged human being with his own desires and interests,
meant that we—my wife and I—usually arrived at a kind of silent
consensus on a method of raising our son that, as I've tried to explain, was really a continual reinforcement of the status quo that
the two of us had long observed, with little thought as to whether
that status quo in any way benefitted our son. This consensus, this
reinforcement of the status quo, then led, in a somewhat hidden

way—hidden, I mean, from us, my wife and me, in that we refused to acknowledge our true motivations, our true cravenness
and laziness—to a set of actions that probably didn't make much
sense to those around us, and some of which actions may have
even struck people as needlessly cruel to our son, or which actions
might have seemed to make trouble for us with regards to him, or
which actions were instead simply (but totally) incomprehensible
to those others (I'm sure this in fact describes the vast majority of
our actions, and not only those undertaken in the course of raising
our son but also really *all* of our actions as a couple when looked
at by those without a stake in their consequences, or rather, those
without a stake in the reinforcement of the status quo, that is to
say, those who don't see that carrying on in the way one has already
been going represents not just the easiest way forward but also, frequently, the *only* way forward, at least, in the view of those asked to
truly consider it). Our way of raising our son was, I mean, or seems
now, with the benefit of hindsight, a series of demands to conform
to the ways my wife and I had worked out of living *with each other
and the world*, asking him to fit into the various compromises we'd
made as we'd learned to live together with each other, the various
temporary arrangements that had, slowly but inevitably, become
long-term (though also unmanageable, because they were never
meant to be long-term) arrangements. Every time we told him he
couldn't do things the way he'd tried to do them, or the way he
wanted to do them—*because we said so*—I became a little more
aware of this pattern in our attitude toward him and our irresponsible or unthinking or even dangerous way of raising him.

   I had, anyway, I thought, chosen Hugbee for my son's head for
an obvious and justifiable reason: Though Hugbee was, clearly, a
teddy bear, it had, as I've already said, a very human face. Thinking
about it, it was, I think, the absence of anything truly ursine in
Hugbee's face, a face that, based on the body below it, was clearly
meant to be a bear's, that always caused a kind of fright—a feeling, I mean, stronger and more pronounced than simple disgust
or dislike—in me. There was no discernible snout, for one thing,

and the eyes were not beady, and the ears were on the sides of the head and not the top of it, and the whole of the face was not especially hairy or fuzzy, and so it really resembled only a person, not so much a bear, and this resemblance to a person was, for me, upsetting, though for my son, it was, very possibly—we'd never talked about it; it's not as though we could have had a conversation of that kind, as young as he was, and anyway I was worried about upsetting my son by trying to explain that his favorite stuffed animal, his constant companion, this thing that I was, daily, made to find or retrieve or even sometimes deprive him of for the purposes of washing it, this Hugbee was upsetting, even frightening, to me—this set of features was, I mean, the very thing that made Hugbee attractive to my son, the very thing that made it *Hugbee*. Given that it had been the first thing my wife had tried to get rid of when we'd begun cleaning out his room, I have to believe that my dislike or unease about Hugbee was shared between us (and likewise the sacrifice or forbearance it had taken to keep the thing around for so long; and this thought made me once again weep, thinking of my wife and her way of being in the world)—and so I think I thought that by using it as his head I would be, in a way, attempting a kind of homeopathy or therapy, or anyway, for once, acting as my son would have wanted me to act rather than in the way that I or my wife wanted me to act so as to teach my son how to act in order to better accommodate himself to life with us. I found I still had trouble meeting Hugbee's eyes, but I thought—I really, truly thought—that using Hugbee in this way could be considered a step forward, towards, I mean, both actually considering and also, finally, implementing my son's wishes and desires, rather than, I mean, asking him to be patient and to accept that my wife and I, despite all of the mistakes we'd made, knew better how to live, how to go forward, when, clearly, we didn't.

And then there's the matter of his legs, which I knew didn't need to be functional and yet which I nevertheless couldn't abide being so completely ornamental as to not be capable of some rough articulation, and which desire, I thought—a conclusion I'm reluctant to draw but can't avoid drawing—pointed, at least possibly, to a set of motivations I'm not ready to completely own. I didn't, in other words, want to give my son rigid legs, incapable of human or human-like motion, but I couldn't find, among his few belongings I'd saved from my wife's purge, anything that fit the description or that would, in any way, fulfill the function I'd imagined for it. It was clear I'd have to make something to purpose, but then this posed a problem, because, now that this project had taken on this shape, I wanted to finish making this figure of my son out of things that had some connection to him, and something made to purpose, a set of legs I found somewhere else, I remember thinking, wouldn't have such a connection, and then I hit on a solution.

In Which

He Describes, in Some Detail, Making a Pair of Legs from the Parts of a Bed

Though we'd arranged to have a charity pick up our son's bed (the pick-up I'd scheduled after my wife threatened to put the bed out by the curb—what did she care what I thought the neighbors would think? I was wrong; they wouldn't think anything other than it was strange that we'd waited so long to get rid of it—was, I remember, first delayed a week because, the charity said, their delivery/hauling crew had been shot at by someone on another pick-up (my wife read this post, from the woman with the police scanner's timeline, to me aloud one night while we ate dinner, I remember—one of the two men on the crew was an ex-con apparently, who'd earlier been convicted of sexual assault and assault with a deadly weapon and who'd been shot before, though neither he nor his partner were hit when they were shot at during the pick-up), then the new pick-up date came and neither my wife nor I was at home, then the re-rescheduled date came and went without anyone showing up at all, and so I'd called again and the charity told me they weren't taking donations of furniture at that time, that the most recent storm had damaged the roof of their warehouse and they encouraged me to give the bed to *someone in need*, as though this were not what they purported to have been founded to do; I of course reported none of this to my wife, hoping that the subject would, for a time anyway, between us, be dropped, and it was dropped, apart from an occasional remark about the charity's negligence that was supposed to remind me, I knew, that giving the bed away was something for which I was responsible, and these hints were also warnings that, if nothing happened soon, she would take the matter into her own hands), the bed was the only one of my son's things still in his room, already taken apart and shoved against the wall under the spot where I had once and was now again supposed to hang my clothes (I had so far refused to do this, refused to accept the room had once again become our closet, even though my wife had already moved her things back in, her dresses and slacks and shirts hanging up on the bar we'd once long ago taken down to convert the room into his bedroom and which bar, after it had become clear I wasn't going to put it back up, was only going to tell my wife I was going to put it back up, never actually putting it back up, my wife had put back up). Now, now that the walls and the floor had been painted, I could move the bed into the garage, I thought, and maybe then it wouldn't seem so empty, and anyway it would be out of my wife's way and also, I hoped, out of mind. Instead, after I'd picked up the two rails, one in each hand so that I wouldn't have to make an extra trip, and carefully negotiated my way through the doorway into our bedroom and then out into the hall and into the living room and out of the house, I decided on a different course.

When it came to these rails, I knew that of course I wouldn't be able to manage anything so sculpted and round as prostheses; I doubted, with my few woodworking skills, I could even manage anything remotely resembling a real human leg, with its diverging slopes of calf and thigh, no matter how much time or effort I expended (I thought of a Pinewood Derby car I'd made when I was a Boy Scout, of how long and hard I'd worked on it, and then seeing it at the top of the track in its own lane, next to the other boys' cars in their lanes, so much more like *cars* than my own almost Charlie-Brown-shoe-shaped thing, feeling completely defeated even before the den mother let it go and it smashed into the side of the lane and skidded slowly down the incline almost sideways). After I'd considered what was possible with the wood chisel, hammer, and jigsaw I'd found in the pawn shop closest to us, still a very long walk away—I'd asked the clerk to take the pistol out of the case, but then, after I'd heard the sound of it being laid on the glass display counter and looked more closely at the thing for a moment, I asked him to please just put it back, and then of course I felt guilty for wasting his time, so I bought the tools (even though the chisel was rusty and the jigsaw's handle looked like someone or something had gnawed on it, and even though, all together, they'd been the same price as the pistol). I thought of a Pinocchio doll I'd once had, with its matchstick-shaped legs—maybe, I later thought, it was the color of the paint on the bed, the red somehow reminding me of his outfit. I thought I could probably do something like that doll's legs, since, in theory, it wouldn't be any more difficult than cutting down one of the rails and then sanding each side of it until I had something like a long cuboid (though that of course still didn't solve the problem of how to attach whatever resulted to the egg, or of how to craft feet to fit, or of how to attach those feet to the legs) and then cutting that cuboid into two equal pieces, one for each leg. The bed had been something we'd bought at one of the big box stores, believing after all it wouldn't need to last long, since the boy would outgrow it within a year or two (along with his room, and all of us the house), at which point we'd have to buy something bigger (and this, this perfect and absolute necessity had been, I admit, weighing on me at the time, and I thought I'd probably convinced my wife against her better judgment to go with this, the cheaper, smaller bed, in part also because it would fit in his room, which would mean we wouldn't need to look for another place to live right away, not seriously, even though she was concerned about the glue that had been used in putting together the pressboard, even showing me the sticker with the words *California law* and *cancer* on it).

I remember the soothing feeling of running the sandpaper along one of the rails, smoothing the splintered wood, hoping the rail wouldn't split and wondering what it would mean if it did, wondering, too, what it meant that I was trying to remake something in the image of my son out of all of these mass-produced parts (baseball glove, stuffed animal, action figure, flat-pack furniture), and so also thinking that it wasn't the fact of their having been mass-produced but rather the fact that they'd been associated with my son that, I thought, made them appropriate, but I remained concerned that I'd chosen the bed's rails because, like the glove, like the wrestler, they simply presented themselves, were most readily available, in other words, and not because they were the most appropriate materials for the job. The wood underneath the paint was soft to the touch and almost springy, seeming as though it had been soaked even though it wasn't appreciably wet, and it was much lighter in color than the paint had been—candy apple red, because the bed was supposed to be a sports car, and sports cars, everyone apparently knew, were always painted candy apple red—in fact, the wood underneath was almost perfectly white, almost seeming not to be wood at all but instead an especially dense kind of paper. Although the surface was very soft, there was also still a solidness to the wood, some core or accumulated thickness that gave the thing shape and weight. I thought this wood could work, but then later that day, after the police came by to ask about the three dead bodies at the homeless camp down by the railroad tracks—*Did you know the man who broke into your home was believed to have lived there? Have there been any other suspicious people in the neighborhood lately?* (and given our recent history with the police, this was, of course, a ridiculous question, though I didn't say so to the officers, who, I thought, would have every right to be suspicious of me, especially if I started mouthing off or told one of my stories in response, even though they weren't the officers I'd dealt with in either of my most recent incidents) *Anyone you've seen going down to the camp?*—I again worried I'd just chosen the rails because they were easy, because, I mean, they were there.

I wouldn't have known I needed to carve a kind of horn at the lower end of the top half of each leg—so that the knees would have a stop built into them and would only swing backwards, in the natural direction, in other words, and not in both directions—if

I hadn't watched a video online made by a man with a strong southern Appalachian accent (in my head, while I worked, I remember I sometimes found myself pronouncing Pinocchio in the dolorous way he had). I remember thinking it was strange that this man—an older man, older than my own father—had so many toys in his workshop, and not just wooden toys but all kinds of toys, including a disturbing arrangement of dolls the cameraman kept cutting to to signal a commercial break was coming and a basket of older unclothed plastic toys, some of which looked very familiar to me from my own childhood. This man's Pinocchio's legs had the horn—really, just a little nub, rounded and smoothed to look like a kneecap; I knew I would never be able to make anything so polished or natural-looking—but they were also fairly loose, and that gave his doll a kind of ragdoll lifelessness I wanted to avoid if possible (the man's toy was meant to at least simulate being a puppet, while what I wanted would be, I thought, fairly stationary and demanded seriousness). Fortunately, the man brought up the issue of the weight of the wood during his video, and so, before I got too far in, I realized I would also have to keep the total mass down so that my son's legs wouldn't pull out and through the egg of their own weight. I drilled all the way through each piece with the smallest bit I could find—still, though, not especially small, I thought—hollowing them out and reducing the weight but also, of course, making them much more fragile in the process, and I remember finding this particularly difficult to do, to focus on, and I remember being especially worried about keeping the drill straight but still not wanting to bother with a more involved—but also more stable—system of vises and clamps, really just wanting to get through it before I started crying, even if it meant making a mistake I couldn't correct. I'd closed my eyes, involuntarily, as though flinching, a few times, and, after I'd very nearly drilled through the outer wall of what would be his right leg, I had to continually remind myself to keep my eyes open so that I wouldn't make any worse mistakes.

For the same reason, wanting to get it over with, I decided I could or in any case would live with two identical legs, even after I'd spent an entire afternoon trying to somehow angle the cuts evenly so that I'd end up with one right leg and one left leg, mirrored images of each other. The next morning, as I cut down the rails with the guide box the man in the video had shown me how to make, I remember thinking that, once again, I was compromising my son's happiness to make accommodations for my own incapacities and impatience, and this was of course not a surprise but still I was discouraged, and, although I was already at the point of planing and sanding the wood I'd cut, I'd thought seriously about giving up, even though I was really very nearly done, and then I noticed that something in the wood was coming to the surface.

Maybe, I remember thinking, because the bed had been made of pressed wood, this was simply the glue that had held the many chips and splinters together beading up now at the surface; it was a clear gel-like liquid, tacky but not exactly like glue, at least, not like any glue I was familiar with—it was more fluid than that, never completely drying but remaining slightly malleable and somewhat sticky—and, as it solidified or anyway as it stilled, it settled like tiny bubbles on the white wood until I'd sanded away the surface on which it had settled, leading to more of the stuff coming up to the surface, and after I'd done this several times, I realized it would keep coming up each time I sanded the wood, and so I'd simply have to live with a certain number of these bubbles on the surface or I'd wind up sanding all the way down to the hollow core.

When the hinges were on and both pieces of the legs were attached to each other, the knees worked more or less as I'd hoped they would, though, like the ones in the video, they swung, I thought, much too freely, and so I gathered some of the sawdust that had come from the wood I'd sanded to remove the wood sweat or glue or whatever it had been, added a little more of that wood sweat or glue or whatever it was to it, and applied that mixture to the hinges, just a very light coating of it, and that seemed to do the trick and hide, at least a little, the shiny metal of the hinges, though this also meant that the knees would sometimes lock in what looked like awkward or uncomfortable positions. I was, in other words, once again trading a certain expediency for the hard work of an actual solution, but, I thought, I couldn't help what I was able to achieve—this had never been very much, I knew, and never quite enough—and then later I thought that this was really the problem: I was unwilling to change myself even when it was clear that if I didn't, others would be hurt.

There were two pairs of his shoes in the box of things I'd saved, or really one and a half pairs: an unmatched right shoe with a light in the heel he'd never worn because it was too big and the pair of shoes he'd worn in the picture we still had of him on the mantle in the living room, one of the few pictures of him my wife had allowed to remain on display in the house, maybe because it had been a picture we'd had taken on the spur of the moment, at a kiosk in the mall, when, as I recall, our son had been crying and furious because we'd denied him some thing—not a toy, though it's possible he'd thought it was a toy, but some thing that we'd decided was unsuitable for such a small child, probably some sort of kitchen gadget or piece of decoration, something we felt certain he wouldn't actually play with even if, for no other reason than to stop him from a meltdown, we bought it for him—and my wife, because she was and had always been much savvier about these things, had decided that *that*, that exact moment, was the right moment to have our picture taken. I remember it had seemed like a strange decision to me, though, once we'd arranged ourselves in front of the camera, our son completely calmed down and my wife, as I see every time I pass the picture, was beaming, though I don't think it was out of a sense of triumph so much as one of relief, or maybe it had been some other feeling I had no access to. I, on the other hand, had an anxious or worried look on my face, probably because I thought another eruption was and always would be in-evitable, and because I knew I wouldn't be up to the task when it came. I thought I could even see my worry about what I would be asked to do when my son threw another tantrum—which he always seemed to do at times that would be most embarrassing for me, when I would have to be the one to correct or discipline him in front of strangers (my wife would then, naturally, criticize the way I'd spoken to him as being either much too strong or else much too lenient, even when I thought my tone had been appropriate—and surely there were times when my wife felt my tone was appropriate, though I couldn't remember even a single one of these times, which I think must be a failure of my memory and perhaps a sign of my feelings affecting my memory rather than a reflection of reality—because of course she would say nothing at all if it had been an appropriate tone, but, as I say, I couldn't remember any such occasion). Given my wife's obvious pleasure and the look of sincere amusement on my son's face in the picture, these shoes, very small black Vans slip-ons, I decided, would work well for his feet. I made two slits around the ankles of the shoes, ran the wire I'd found in the drawer with my wife's craft things through those slits, then clamped the wire tight around the square knobs at the ends of the lower legs.

This representation of my son was then complete, though I remember, strangely, I found no sense of accomplishment or triumph in this fact, mainly because, at the time, I couldn't think of what exactly to do with him; it wasn't as though my work in the garage had changed my relationship with my wife (she still didn't know anything about it), and there was really no one else to show it off to, so, a few days later (and at the end of each of these days, I always had trouble deciding what to do with my son, whether to set him on top of the box on the shelf, which seemed much too high up for him—what if he fell?—or else to put him on the worktable, even with all the sawdust and wood glue or sweat there, which seemed disrespectful somehow, and I compromised by putting the box of his things on the worktable and setting him somewhat inside it, though this meant that each morning, when I picked him up out of it, I could feel how fragile he was and worried I was doing damage to his torso in particular), I finally did the only thing I could think to do: I arranged the headboard and the footboard of the bed as they would have stood if the bed had been put together and, with some galvanized ell-shaped brackets I bought at the hardware store, I attached both of them to the peg-board, at what I thought was an appropriate distance from each other, so that, although the rails were gone, looked at from certain angles, it almost seemed as though the bed had been put back together. I then removed the legs of the worktable and cut it in half so that it would fit between the headboard and the footboard, more or less like a mattress, nailed it to the headboard and footboard, covered the table in one of my son's blankets, and placed my son on the table, as though he were sitting up in bed, waiting for a story before going to sleep.

In Which

He Explains the Matter

My wife and I had, when he was alive, disagreed about many things when it came to our son, and this general situation—this larger set of disagreements—in turn led to a number of further disagreements, on really a whole range of matters, disagreements that continually flared up in any number of circumstances and often at the most unfortunate and awkward moments. I don't want to give the wrong impression: It's not that I'm saying that our son was the cause of our arguments—I don't think anyone who saw the situation the way it actually was would deny that his birth (and really even my wife's pregnancy) aggravated things a great deal, but, even so, he wasn't the *cause* of any of it; after all, my wife and I had had bitter disagreements long before his birth, as I'm sure all couples do—no, it's just that, after his birth, these disagreements grew substantially worse and more frequent, and this in fact got worse as he got older. My wife and I had long had difficulties coming together on important decisions—I think this was, usually, because we both feared the other's disapproval, and so one or the other of us would simply refuse to give their opinion, holding back until the other had finally said something all so that the one who hadn't yet suggested anything could then declare that, no, that wasn't the thing to do, that couldn't be the only good option, in fact it wasn't a good option at all, here were all the reasons why it was a bad option, here were the outcomes that were most likely (all bad), here were all the problems with that way of doing things, and then this person, myself or my wife, could say and think all of this with a clear conscience, all while still declining to actually offer an

181

alternative of any kind—and, at just the moment when we started making decisions for another person, for our son, I think we both realized the full weight of the responsibility we'd taken on, and we both (though now I realize that I must have felt this more acutely than did my wife) felt completely inadequate to the task, and this made things much more contentious between us.

The bowl was as good an example of this as any; once my wife had begun the process by claiming she didn't care what we did, whatever we decided to do would be fine but we ought to do *something* to replace the broken bowl, we couldn't just leave things as they were, *something* would have to be found to replace it, whether that meant getting another bowl or not, and, seeing that it would be left to me to make the first suggestion about what exactly that meant, what we'd replace the bowl with, I—because I couldn't help it; I know that, if I'd thought about it longer, even for a few minutes, I wouldn't have said anything at all (but then, I knew, my wife would have been angry with me for staying silent, I thought)—I said *Well, we could have tried to put the bowl back together if we hadn't thrown away the pieces.* I mean, there were very small bits that had completely shattered—slivers, really, nothing too much larger—but for the most part, I'd thought, it would have been possible (with, obviously, a lot of care and focus, an amount of care and focus I'd never had, or that we—my wife and I—had never as a couple had, but, still, I thought, *possible*). I'd known when I said this that, because she was the one who'd thrown those bits away—I'd put them all in a paper bag that I then placed at the end of the kitchen counter where it sat for two or three weeks before it was thrown away, and even though I looked up *best glue for ceramics* on my phone (the tab is still open in the browser), I never actually began the process of gluing the bowl back together because of course even then I knew that the sooner I started that process, the sooner I'd realize how terrible the bowl looked when glued back together—because, in other words, she was responsible for closing off this particular solution to the problem, she'd see this (probably correctly) as me blaming her for our failure to replace the bowl. Besides which, a glued-together bowl was completely unacceptable: *It won't look the same*, she'd said. *It'll look tacky.* She meant, I knew, that the bowl, back in its place, would look as though it had been broken and then repaired, that the evidence of its having once been broken would be all anyone saw—and my poor repair job would be perfectly obvious, though she didn't say this and didn't need to—and so, in effect, she was saying that this solution wasn't really a solution at all and shouldn't be considered, not seriously. At the time, I think I tried to seem as though I really had no stake in the matter—I was perfectly happy to have the sideboard stand empty, or, not empty, but full of mail—but then my wife complained that I wasn't taking her seriously, that the bowl was just an example of this more serious and more general problem in our relationship, and so, suddenly, in that moment, it wasn't the bowl we were disagreeing about but our life together, the entire thing, and so, with misgivings (by which I mean: knowing I was setting myself up to fail), I said, *Well, maybe we can find another one like it.* I pulled out my phone, and, after struggling to remember the name of the style of this bowl—which, after all, we hadn't ourselves bought but been gifted—I found what looked to me, from what I could remember, like the same bowl on sale at Macy's.

What I'd meant to explain, in going back into all of this, is the general shape of the relationship my wife and I had, whether our son was involved in what we were discussing or not. There was, for instance, the matter of his crib, before he'd even been born, and his bassinet, and his Pack-N-Play, and his car seat, and even his clothes—each of these things was subject to second-, third-, and fourth-guessing, though really what this second-, third-, and fourth-guessing amounted to was a series of attacks on the other person for one's own frustrations, anxieties, and feelings of inadequacy, or so I remember feeling at the time. I'd brought this up after he was born, when we were looking at beds to replace his crib, more or less completely out of a spontaneous impulse—it was a thought I'd had for some time, but I'd always known better than to bring it up out loud, and then, suddenly, with my wife telling me, *But that bed's too big for him. He'll fall out of it at night. He could be seriously hurt. You're not even listening to me!* (she'd included the *You're not even listening to me!* because I—in what I'd thought was a perfectly reasonable answer to the criticism *that bed's too big for him*—had suggested that we get a smaller bed instead, at which point my wife reminded me of an earlier conversation we'd had in which we'd considered and rejected a series of smaller beds, first because of their obvious shoddiness and second because such a bed would need to be replaced in less than a year, when he'd outgrown it, and the expense of not only the bed in the moment but also of the bed's replacement; in other words, that we'd be, in effect, buying two beds if we chose the smaller option; I had, apparently, agreed—the criticisms had been, I was informed, *mine*, at least, originally), as a result, I mean, of feeling attacked on what had seemed to me, at the time, a trivial matter—there were more important things to worry about, I didn't say; there was my always-tenuous employment to consider and the pressure I was under to produce some publishable scholarship because the department's politicking was working against me, I'd wanted to say. There was the state of our relationship, the state of the world around us, I'd wanted to say, and, because I couldn't help myself, these things came out.

We differed, mainly or most strongly—though reducing things down to a single category like this is probably really only foolishly producing a horribly inaccurate caricature when one has after all intended to paint a complete and faithful portrait—on how to discipline our son, which is to say, I think, that neither one of us really wanted to discipline him at all; not that we didn't often get frustrated with him or wish he didn't do things differently (or, worse, see a future in which he acted in a way that reflected poorly on our so-called *parenting skills*), just that, when faced with punishing him or forcing him to follow rules, I think we both just *wanted* him to act differently, as though he could learn to do so without our intervention, as inhumane or despicable as that must sound. Not (not exactly) that we didn't want to *be the bad guy* or anything like that, just that we didn't want the responsibility, and ultimately, we didn't want to look back on those moments and see ourselves in the faces of those ugly parents telling their child to act his age, to stop doing whatever it was that he was doing, to do what we said, not what we did, not to climb over the gate, if he couldn't see us, we couldn't see him. For me, there was a sense that, because I couldn't think of myself as an authority on anything—I knew better than to think that—it was difficult for me to act with authority without also feeling as though I'd harmed myself in some way, as though I was, as a result, making myself more inauthentic and so less myself, a kind of assault on the core of my being. I don't know why my wife found it difficult, though I'd guess at least part of her reticence came, in fact, from my inaction—I mean that she may have been waiting for me to act simply so that she wouldn't always have to be the one to act, so that our son (and I) didn't think that that was the way things always ought to work—always *did* work—meaning, I guess, that she didn't want to be seen as merely inhabiting a role any more than I did, wanted, that is, to remain a human being, an individual, liable to act in many different and sometimes contradictory ways. I couldn't fault her for this, and there were moments when I felt she was waiting for me to act, when I knew I was expected to act, and yet in which moments I held back, thinking—to my own great shame—that I couldn't act, couldn't make the obvious decision, precisely because I was being counted upon to make exactly that decision. Though that may seem unnecessarily antagonistic, I'm not sure that it was, or, actually, at the time, I remember I felt certain that it *wasn't*. In those moments—if he fell, he fell; he would get back up; I'd broken so many bones when I was a kid, had so many accidents, and I was fine—especially when I held back or refused to make the obvious decision, I felt as though I was being the bigger person, by which I mean I felt I was taking the blame for not acting so that my wife or my son could have the opportunity to exercise their own agency, taking on a responsibility they might not otherwise have had. Though I'm conscious that this sounds bad—self-serving, I mean, in an unflattering way—I felt as though in not making those decisions, I was also, in my own way, doing them a service, no matter how frustrating those situations might have been for them in the moment (and I have no doubt they were frustrating), and these were all things that, much later and after the day of the eclipse and of course many other things had happened, my wife told me had influenced her decision to first make the appointment with the lawyer I'd found in her daybook and then to keep that appointment, and then, after it had become clear that there were no other options left, to tell me I ought to find my own lawyer.

In Which
He Explains About the Car

Shortly before that, though—before, I mean, my wife and I had that conversation and before the day of the eclipse—we had a conversation about her car, or, really, we had a conversation about the fact that she *didn't have* a car, not one she could drive, and obviously she couldn't (*wouldn't*) drive mine, and so the conversation we were having was less about her car than it was about her getting a car, which is then to say that the conversation we were having was about the loan we'd have to get in order for her to get the car. The car my wife was driving was the rental provided to us by the insurance company, a PT Cruiser whose handling, my wife said, was strangely both *stiff* and *mushy*—these were the words she used—and whose tiny rear window was, as far as I could tell, just a blind spot behind glass; through the rearview mirror, my wife said, it looked like the back window of a very small pick-up truck with three or four mattresses piled up in the bed. I can remember that she'd said this car was *untenable*, that she couldn't drive it much longer—not safely, and anyway, the insurance wouldn't keep paying for it—and so she'd already started looking at cars on eBay and Craigslist.

A new car had become necessary through a variety of circumstances. First, of course, had been our next-door neighbor, who, after the second of the spring's tropical storms, lost the live oak along the property line, and who'd afterward developed an intense passion for tree-trimming, which resulted in a very large dent on the hood of my wife's car, a cracked windshield, and the front bumper coming loose, but, after all, he'd fallen out of the tree and the same limb that landed on the car also landed on him, and so we'd felt bad about suing him even though the insurance company claimed they'd only pay for the repairs if we took the car to a mechanic who had, my wife told me, nearly ruined one of her coworkers' cars when he reinstalled a belt incorrectly, because, the insurance agent said, this mechanic was *preferred* (really what was meant, I knew, was that the other mechanics the company had once contracted with had all closed for lack of business after the hurricanes or wanted more money than the insurance company was willing to pay them), and my wife refused to do this, and our neighbor's homeowner's policy didn't cover it, but then we couldn't sue him because his wife had, by then, left him and there was also the matter of his broken legs and the fact that, with his wife gone and him not able to get around, he would also, in what seemed likely to be short order, lose his business (he and his one employee paved and painted the stripes on parking lots, a business it had never occurred to me was a business until he'd told us about it, and which business, for lack of new stores, restaurants, and offices in town, I remember thinking even then, was probably doomed to fail anyway), and so there would be nothing for us to recoup even if we won the suit, and anyway we'd still have to live next to him, at least until we found another place to live. Still, the car had been badly damaged, and it had clearly been his fault. And then the more serious accident happened: A garbage truck backed into my wife's car while it was parked in front of our house (she'd been getting around by asking her friends to drive her places), while my wife and I were inside, arguing about how much of our son's stuff I was trying to keep and where I was going to put it—the point was that she wouldn't have to keep seeing it, she was saying, and the more I tried to keep, the more likely it was she'd see it, or the more of it there was for her to see. There was no question as to who was at fault; the truck had been backing up because it had just hit the building on the corner, a gas station that had closed long before we'd moved into the neighborhood and which, because of its long vacancy, had, apparently, become a squat. The truck hadn't only run into the building, breaching the cinder block wall, but also, because those cinder blocks had fallen in on a couple squatting there, the driver, it turned out, had killed two people. He later claimed that he'd been crying at the time, and so his vision had been impaired, and he thought he'd seen someone run out into the street and had swerved to miss this person, though the police, according to the woman with the police scanner's post later that week, never found any such person, and this same woman—who sent my wife a private message offering legal help and the number of a *good lawyer*, one, my wife told me, whose name and number were on a dozen billboards around town—posted that this person had been made up; in fact, she wrote, there were rumors that the driver was addicted to painkillers and had known the squatters, but I don't know if there was any truth to those rumors. I think, anyway, I was more interested in the detail that he'd been crying, and wondered why he'd been crying, as anyone would, though I also felt strongly that any explanation this driver gave would sure-ly have been only some lie he'd made up, either on purpose or through his natural and very human inability to see things as they were. We'd heard the truck hit the gas station and then we'd heard the truck hit my wife's car, and because we didn't want to have the argument we were then having, we'd both gone out to the street to look.

The truck, in backing up, had hit the front axle of my wife's car, and, because there was no bumper because of the tree branch, the impact bent it so much the tow-truck driver told us the car would be undrivable even if we replaced the windshield and ham-mered out the body, and so my wife—who refused even to get into my car and who, after I stopped driving it, insisted I park it down the block, in front of one of the abandoned houses—informed me that I could keep saying we ought to just take her car to the *pre-ferred* mechanic all I wanted, but she was going to get a new one. The question, in other words, was no longer whether she would get a new car or fix the old one—it was obvious she'd need a new car— it was whether she would apply for financing by herself or with me, and whether the title would be entirely under her name or shared with me. And even these questions might never have come up if, for reasons I didn't then understand, she hadn't, some months before, stopped paying a series of medical bills issuing from our son's last visit to the hospital. She later told her lawyer, in one of the proceedings, that it was because they (the bills) just never stopped coming, this unending series of painful reminders of an event she really didn't want to be reminded of—first the orthopedic surgeon sent her bill, then the pediatric surgeon his, and then the hospital itself, and then the paramedics, and then the anesthesiologist, and so on and so on and so on, each little bit coming in some time after the last had been paid off, which only happened after the bill had first been shoved under a pile of other bills and papers, so that she could at least *try* to forget about it for a time, and, not that any of it was her responsibility, at least, not *solely* her responsibility (not really her responsibility at all, and the fact that she felt some guilt over the situation was itself a sign of her extraordinary kindness to me), but she'd insisted, long before all of this, that she could take on the responsibility of paying our bills on time (and this, I can remember, had been the result of a previous argument from years before—again, she remembered these kinds of things in detail— about her lack of responsibility that had arisen from an argument we'd had about our son's schedule (she had realistic priorities and I had unreasonable expectations and if sometimes he ate later or napped earlier, he'd still be fine, he didn't mind, *I* was the one who minded, my feelings were just that, *my feelings*, nothing objective or authoritative after all)), and so I'd handed over those responsibilities to her (and, afterwards, of course, I knew better than to ask whether certain bills had been paid, because, inevitably, when I asked whether she'd done something she should have done, she'd tell me it wasn't time yet, she would do it—which meant, obviously, she *hadn't* done it yet, and both she and I realized this—and she didn't appreciate me treating her like she couldn't handle something this small and insignificant when, after all, her job involved a great deal more stress and responsibility than mine did, or at least as she had come to characterize my job as having). Anyway, because of the way we'd structured our finances—a result of her father's advice; he was a lawyer—her credit had been affected by these various delinquencies, but mine hadn't, not yet, and so of course there was the trade-off of getting a better, more affordable deal on the financing if I were a co-signer or of finally being done with me altogether if I were not.

But ultimately what I set out to say was that at several points during this conversation about the new car and financing the new car I had a strong impulse to pull my wife up off the couch and bring her out to the garage with me, to show her what I'd done, without saying a word of explanation about what we were going to do or why we were going to do it, but, in the end and because of the way she was talking to me, I couldn't manage it. When it had become clear to both of us that what we were really discussing in that moment (and this preceded her recommendation that I get a lawyer), not financing, not the wisdom of co-signing or the importance of rebuilding her credit, not even the car itself but *severance*, an end to something that had now gone on so long it seemed impossible to end it voluntarily, I could feel how strongly (physically, I mean) she would resist me if I grabbed her hand, her arm, how strongly she would resist even my touch, maybe even the motion on my part to get closer to her, most especially if it involved standing above her, and so instead I did nothing even as I felt, almost throughout the entire conversation, and especially after it had become clear to me what we were really discussing, on the point of pulling her up. I'm not certain that I thought showing her the garage would solve anything—certainly it had no relevance whatsoever to the subject of her new car, to financing or independence—I think it's more likely that I simply thought it was anyway the best answer (the best answer *at this point*) that I could make to such an important, unasked question as the one we were really, in that moment, working ourselves up to finally asking each other.

He Describes Yet Another Dream, This One More Disturbing

The night before this conversation, I dreamed—and even thinking about this now is difficult—that my son hadn't died, that he'd continued to grow up and grow older, even though, in the dream, I remember that I seemed to be the same age I am now; I'd remained the same age, and he'd grown older, and, although, obviously, I didn't know what he'd look like when he was older—or what he *would have* looked like, I guess I should say, if he'd lived—I nevertheless knew, without question, that he was my son, and, because, in the dream, he was older and more mature, his face and his overall appearance had finally left that state of limbo in which he'd existed when he actually was alive and with us, that state in which, depending on which angle you looked at him from, he looked just like me when I was his age, or just like his mother when she was his age, or just like my father, or just like my wife's brother, and, in the dream, he had, in other words, become more fully himself, but still he looked like me, looked like my wife. He was, I mean, in the dream, both deeply familiar and also strange, like what a childhood friend whom one hasn't seen since early childhood might look like thirty years later—with features, in other words, that I recognized immediately, but also with features that seemed not to belong to him, as though they'd been pressed into him or onto him and hadn't quite set, like he was wearing a set of clothes that belonged to someone else, someone of a very different size and shape, or maybe like he was wearing a silicone mask identical in almost all ways to the face underneath the mask. One of the strangest things about this dream was that I could see myself, also, as though from outside my own body, but *not* as though I were some other person looking at me and my son; what I mean is, in the dream, I wasn't inhabiting some other body, and I didn't feel disconnected from myself, but I could, nonetheless, look at myself from outside of myself. I don't know if this had anything to do with my son being older (or, I guess, my own dream-agelessness), but I've thought, since then, that the two things might somehow have been related, and I often think of them together—though that doesn't mean I've come up with any idea of what they have to do with each other.

It's a painful dream to remember, though it was also a short dream, and I think if it weren't so painful, I might not remember it, or might not think of it as often as I do, but I do, I think of it often. In the dream, though my son and I don't speak to each other, we're standing together, in my grandfather's cabin, a cabin my grandfather built himself and which cabin, because of the era during which he was building it, when dark wood paneling was in fashion, was paneled entirely in dark wood. The cabin was, also, I remember, a slightly strange shape, not quite plumb in any aspect—my grandfather was a mortician, not an engineer or an architect, so the cabin, while it looked, from the porch, perfectly ordinary, as soon as one stepped inside, one realized that something was off, that the foreshortening of perspective was especially strong and the room (there was only one) seemed to get narrower with each step you took toward the galley kitchen in the back, and this feature of the cabin was exaggerated in the dream, so that, by the time we stood in what was, in real life, the kitchen, next to the wood-burning stove, the room was only just barely wide enough for the both of us to stand next to each other, shoulder to shoulder. My son and I are there, in the cabin, and there's a film of dust on everything that keeps getting kicked up by our movements, though it isn't, in the dream, as though either one of us is moving around much, and both of us are being basically respectful of the stillness, which is to say we're both moving slowly and carefully in this fog of dust. There's the sound of the cicada, of course, but otherwise everything is silent.

Though in the dream I haven't noticed it before this point, the me that I'm seeing looks over his shoulder at my son—and, again, I'm viewing all of this somehow from outside of myself, although I still, in the dream, feel connected to the me that I see—and see that my son is holding a pair of pliers. For some reason, I don't think to say anything, and it's only in retrospect, after I wake up, and then again later in the day, when my wife and I are having our discussion about her car and the financing for that car and when I want very badly to pull her up out of her chair and bring her out to the garage, when I think back on the dream and think that in the dream I ought to have tried to say something at this moment—despite the fact that, at that point, in the dream, I couldn't possibly have known what would happen next—should, I mean, have been in a position to say *I tried to speak, but couldn't*, and I notice that my mind is trying to alter my memory of the dream to make it seem as though this was in fact what happened in the dream, because, after all, what else would a father have done in such a situation, especially upon seeing a son he hasn't seen in so long? I mean that I can sense I'm changing my memory of what I'd dreamt by thinking: *The right thing to have done in the dream is to have tried to speak, even if, in the end, I found I couldn't*, and now, just by thinking this, I'm making myself believe that I may, in fact, have tried to speak in the dream, but I'm also conscious of a doubt, conscious, I mean, that I didn't have any such thought in the dream, and so I retain—but just barely—my sense that, in the dream, I didn't try to speak even though I thought I probably *should* have spoken, and then of course I worry that, in realizing that my mind is trying to change this memory in a self-serving way, and in then resisting that change even though it leads to a less flattering outcome in memory, that I may in fact be acting in a self-serving way anyway, by which I mean, I am, in insisting that, though my mind wants me to think that I tried to speak in the dream but couldn't, also insisting that, in the dream, I wasn't acting myself, wasn't thinking in a compassionate or caring way, and so I am, in thinking this way, trying to absolve my dream-self of any responsibility for what then happened, which is that my son then reached into his mouth with the pliers and began pulling out his teeth, one by one, each with a gush of blood that dribbled down his chin and splattered out onto the wall, dropping each tooth on the floor until he had removed them all, at which point his mouth opened so wide that all of his head above his top lip flopped over backward, as though on a fleshy hinge, and a rabbit popped out of his cracked head, seeming much too large to emerge from the opening, and, in the dream, I was so distraught that I couldn't even move to help it up and out of my son's throat to relieve his distress (his body was shaking, I remember, as though he were regurgitating the rabbit), and then, at that moment in the dream, I woke up, or feel that I must have woken up. I felt, I mean, that what I'd just experienced *must have been a dream*, no matter how realistic it had seemed when I was in it, and as much as what happened in the dream seems to have had an effect on my life outside of the dream, in the way that a thought or a decision or an idea may, even though it really has no real-world equivalent, nevertheless entirely infect reality in such a way as to be, in effect, a real thing, like conspiracies are for the conspiracy-minded, I mean, or as otherwise innocuous behavior may seem to the righteous, still, there was a relief that was, nevertheless, unwelcome and about which I feel shame and guilt.

He Takes Measures

As I think I've already mentioned, the egg I'd used as the torso of the figure in the garage had been dented and damaged before I'd found it next to the next-door neighbor's trashcans, and, when I attached the legs to it, I could see that some sort of insect had been in it, though I'd thought then that it was empty at the time. I'd wanted, then, to fill it in some way, to keep insects and other things out of it and to help it stay roughly the same shape, and, some time that week, a box from my wife's mother arrived, with some dinner plates she'd kept in storage—plates she hadn't needed because of course we had the plates we'd been given after our wedding—and I scooped out what I thought would be enough of the packing foam to fill the egg but not so much my wife would notice it missing, filled the front of my shirt, and went out to the garage. The egg was already cracked around what was supposed to be the thighs, the only places I'd pierced the egg—to attach the legs; both arms and the head were attached only to the shirt—and so, after I'd removed the right leg to access the slit where it joined the body so that I could carefully insert the foam peanuts, one by one, these cracks grew and spread. It was, I remember, the spread of these cracks that, in that moment, made me realize what it was that I'd done, what my wife would see if I showed her this thing I'd spent weeks making. I knew I couldn't possibly show my wife anything so grotesque, and so, not knowing what else to do, I held this figure I'd made as carefully as I could and I cried. She would see the cracks. She would see the clumsy sewing job I'd done to attach the glove to the shirt's sleeve. She would see the stiffness of the knees and the thinness of the legs. She would ask about the egg; was I mocking the memory of our son? Was that what this was? Worse? This was disgusting. How could I do something like this? I was sick.

I picked up the figure very carefully, holding it where the backs of the legs had been inserted into the egg, with Hugbee's face facing outward. The moment I picked it up, I could feel the egg beginning to come apart, beginning to give along the existing cracks. Still, it held together enough that I took a few tentative steps out of the garage, and, feeling I'd passed the threshold and that, whether I continued toward the house, where I thought my wife was, or back into the garage, what was about to happen was going to happen, I continued down the driveway toward the house almost as though I had no control over what I was doing.

My wife, though, wasn't at the table in the kitchen, where I expected her to be. She wasn't in the bedroom or the bathroom. With each step, I could feel that the egg was coming apart in my arms, but it was now too late to turn back, and so I continued to the already-open front door. Outside, I noticed, there was a very curious light, as though a large bank of clouds had covered the sky. I had, though I didn't realize it at the time, forgotten that there was going to be a solar eclipse that day—there'd been so many other things happening that, although there had been a bunch of articles about the eclipse maybe a month or a month and a half ago, since then, it had been pushed out of the headlines in favor of coverage of the latest mass shooting or murder or disaster. Even so, I found my wife standing outside, in the middle of the street, with a pair of paper glasses on her face, next to the neighbor with the Great Danes and the next-door neighbor in his wheelchair, who were both also holding these paper glasses to their eyes and looking up into the sky. I didn't want our neighbors to know what I'd done, but I thought if I turned around, at this point, the egg wouldn't even make it back into the house. The next-door neighbor was, I thought, saying something to my wife about coronas; I couldn't hear him that well, he was speaking very quietly, as though they were all standing together in a museum or a library, speaking so that only my wife and the neighbor with the Great Danes could hear him clearly, and, when I called out to my wife, I realized that it was, for once, completely silent outside—there were no traffic sounds, no construction noise, not even the constant humming of the electrical junction at the end of the block—and it was also, of course, sweltering, and humid, and I was sweating into the egg, through my clothes, and I could feel a kind of warmth coming off it that, in retrospect, now, I'm sure was just the effect of holding this mass of wood pulp, plastic, fabric, leather, and packing materials against me, and that I would have felt the same heat no matter what I'd been carrying, but in that moment, in the moment I first felt that warmth, I recoiled from it just a little, and, when I realized that I'd recoiled, I started to cry again, to gasp and sob. It wasn't grief or sadness that made me cry, though it might have been shame; at the time, though, because there was also a rush of adrenaline that had come with my tears, I thought that the reason for my tears might actually have been terror, the terror of being alive but realizing, as though for the first time, that one day I would be dead. Not sadness, I wanted to think, not grief.

My wife heard me call her name—it was far too quiet for her to pretend, as she sometimes did (as *I* sometimes did when she called out to me), that she hadn't heard me—and she looked down; down, I mean, from the sky, which had now become almost entirely black and seemed endless. I saw stars all of a sudden, probably the result of my eyes finally adjusting to the change in light outside; all this time, from the moment when I stepped into the garage that morning to this moment, now, on the street, standing before my wife and our neighbors, holding our cracking, disintegrating son, it had been getting progressively darker, first because of the clouds, now because of this eclipse, and it had also, it seemed now, been getting progressively quieter, though I'd noticed neither until I'd exited our house and wandered out of the front door, still, now, standing there, the dimness and quiet affected even me, and I felt both the terror I've already described and a kind of awe, I guess, a feeling of being much too small and too weak to be faced with this situation. My wife, as I've said, looked down from the sky, with her cheap paper and plastic glasses, looked at me, at the thing I was carrying, as though looking *through* us at first, maybe simply unable to see us with those glasses on in the sudden twilight. She looked past us, I thought, back at the house behind us, as though I was calling to her from where I'd stood moments before, as though I'd finally somehow moved backward through the past instead of forward, into the future (I had, I realized, become acutely conscious of being dragged forward through time ever since our son died, even though I could see, now, that all of my actions, for as long as I could remember, had always been, at least unconsciously (and sometimes quite consciously), attempts to delay the forward movement of time; all of these attempts were, ultimately, bad for me, of course, bad, in fact, for everyone around me—I'd come to things late, grown up late, put off advancing through time or maturing—but she was the one who'd had to suffer for all of my immature mistakes, like refusing to have children until I was almost forty, or failing utterly to find even a stable job, something, I mean, that could be counted upon from one year to the next, or having been a renter, a transient in my own life, or putting off the hard work of not walking away from my various failures, of having never saved money or invested wisely, never much cared about my health, always made decisions based around what seemed best at that moment to prolong that moment and without regard to what might come out of those decisions—and my wife had been, for months now or maybe I should say for years, forever, giving me clear signs that she was unwilling to stay stuck in this moment with me any longer, and really, I'd long ago ceased to blame her for this unwillingness but still couldn't make myself change; again, though, it isn't like I didn't suspect that all of what I did was really my way of regressing, of trying to go back to what I thought of as a time with less conflict, less strife, more harmony, if only in my own life, a time when, in short, I felt I'd had fewer responsibilities, fewer things that weighed on me, and all of this, this entire

tendency, which was really the ruling philosophy of my life, all of
it seemed to me, in that instant, truly reprehensible, awful, even
monstrous), and I began to sob harder because I could feel that
the egg, in my arms, had now lost one of its legs and was slowly
spilling out white packing foam that was almost the only thing
I could see clearly in the dark, and though I could once again
feel, although much, much stronger this time (fatally, as it seemed
to me, as though having been struck down dead), that sense of
doom, that sense that surely nothing ever again would be right,
nothing ever again would be fixable, nothing ever again would
even be bearable, that I'd almost certainly be lost no matter what I
did next, and I wanted also to sink to my knees (I thought, for the
briefest of instants, that sinking to my knees was really all that I
could possibly do under the circumstances, all that I could possibly
do to show how contrite I was) because I felt, I mean, that my wife,
who was, by then, all that I had left, was finally and forever lost
to me, and because I realized that she was all that I had left, that
everyone else had long ago been lost to me, that, above all, my son
was lost to me, and that sinking to my knees was the only possible
remedy, if only because it would, I thought in that moment, show
that I was truly sorry, that I realized, once and for all, that I was a
monster, that I had nothing, nothing at all, nothing in the least, to
look forward to without her there, and then, suddenly and without
warning, the quiet around us all began to fill with that strident
wheezing sound that had seemed to ebb and flow throughout that
spring and early summer, the noise of the cicadas, and it grew and
grew until it was, finally, deafening, actually deafening, and I felt,
with the first swellings of this noise, a few pinging blows to my
head and my shoulders, even my legs, sharp but brief strikes, so
that I'd been shocked out of my sudden desire to fall to my knees,
and I think really everyone, my wife, our neighbors, everyone must
have felt these shocks, but I couldn't be certain because I couldn't
hear them in the street over the sudden roar of these cicadas, and I
couldn't see them because of the eclipse, and something about the
sound and the darkness and the surprise of being hit, like someone

invisible was flicking me with their finger as hard as they could, over and over again in different spots, actually did finally force me to my knees, and I tried at first to cover the egg, to protect it from whatever it was that was hitting us, but then I realized that, instead of protecting it, I was in fact crushing it under me, and the cracking I felt under me was distinct from the flicking, so that I felt my chest sinking closer and closer to the cement, and out flowed a strange kind of relief, like when water gets into your ear and, after hours of shaking your head, holding it to the side, jumping up and down, finally, finally there is that sudden hot flow, which is really the tiniest little trickle of water, but, because, with it, your hearing returns, it seems like there should be a torrent running down your neck and all it is instead is a few drops that tickle the hairs there, and, in that moment, inside of me, there was something like that, except, instead of hearing returning with it, instead of the small trickle, there seemed to be a flow of something inside me that went on and on, and there was no relief in it; it wasn't absolution, it wasn't even forgiveness, it was just the very slow release of a pent-up tension, and I realized only later, in fact, only now, in describing all of this, that this was really the egg, underneath me, cracking open, and all that I'd stuffed inside it coming out, and some sort of instinctual reaction in me of the realization that my wife would never see what I'd brought to show her, would never see what I'd done, would never know that I'd been laboring in that garage all those weeks for us, really, for both of us, for all three of us, not only for me, but for all of us, for her, for myself, and for our son, and she would, as a result, be able to go on with her life without the horrible burden of seeing it, of seeing me like that, of seeing what I'd done.

Acknowledgments

The author wishes to thank Greg Gerke for his example, for his encouragement, and for featuring an excerpt of *Doom Town* in *Socrates on the Beach*. If not for Jim Gauer, this book would have taken a very different form. Thanks are also due Matt Bell, Brian Evenson, and Jen Craig. Above all, the author wishes to thank his family, without whom there would be no book.

ZEROGRAM PRESS

WEBSITE:
www.zerogrampress.com
EMAIL:
info@zerogrampress.com

Distributed by Small Press United /
Independent Publishers Group
(800) 888-4741 / www.ipgbook.com

*

TITLES

Gabriel Blackwell *Doom Town* 2022
Jen Craig *Panthers and the Museum of Fire* 2020
Steve Erickson *American Stutter* 2022
Hélène Gaudy *A World with No Shore* 2022
Jim Gauer *Novel Explosives* 2016
Greg Gerke *See What I See: Essays* 2021
Rick Harsch *The Manifold Destiny of Eddie Vegas* 2022
Steven Moore *My Back Pages: Reviews and Essays* 2017
    Alexander Theroux: A Fan's Notes 2020
Nicholas John Turner *Hang Him When He Is Not There* 2021